HOUSE OF CUTS

A Hillary Broome Novel

June Gillam

"Calls to mind *Silence of the Lambs* by Thomas Harris."
—Susan Rushton, Columnist, *Auburn Journal*

Published by Gorilla Girl Ink, USA
ISBN 978-0-9858838-1-2

FOR JERRY
WHO LOVED DIA DE LOS MUERTOS

Susan —
Thank you
for your support —
Enjoy the book!
Jerry G.

PART I

October 2005

Revenge is a kind of wild justice.
—*Francis Bacon*

ONE

Mission and Strategy

I SLASHED THE BLACK MARKER one last time across the white paper, perfecting my plan. His flesh and bones would separate under my knife, like I had been parted from my work. Final. Businesslike. Nothing personal. Brookfield was just doing his PriceCuts job—hiring and firing the little people.

After gravity settled his blood below the waist, I'd sever his arms from the shoulders. Then slice through the elbows one at a time. My boning knife would slide right through cartilage. Separate the humerus from the lower arms, give me four pieces. Keep it clean. Place the parts on his desk, palms up, reaching out for money.

I'd stashed a couple twenties in my wallet—twenties seemed the right size, not too big, not too small. Get shoppers to picture the flow of dollars into the retailer's greedy hands.

I would cut off his blond head, leave his torso sitting at the desk, one of the mindless millions serving the global giant. Bring his head home to the basement, save it for later, keep those blue eyes bright in formaldehyde. Keep a couple other parts, too. Come in handy to underscore the message in case folks didn't get it.

Scraping the stool back from the workbench, I lifted up my design and stepped over to the bulletin board. Humming, I tacked the drawing onto the corkboard, stained and stabbed over the years with important papers. Keeping my gaze on the pattern, I backed up to the middle of the room, turned and stretched up to snap on the overhead light bulb. I leaned against the load-bearing post in the center of this space I knew so well. The length of my body relaxed, and I grinned. Let the lessons begin.

Shutting my eyes, I listened for Mother, hoping she'd return and help out. In that dream she'd come back from the dead and whispered that I should apply at the monster store after they forced our little butcher shop out of business.

In the dim, cool space her soft voice chanted: Thou shalt not kill, Thou shalt not kill, Thou shalt not kill.

No. She of all people should see the difference.

Praying her spirit might hear me, I shouted into the silent air: "Some kills are evil, Mother! But this one, it's sacred. Sacred, pristine. Not a drop of blood will I spill."

I listened. Nothing. "You'll be proud of me when you see the clean work and the good it will do."

Turning, I studied her canned goods lining the basement shelves. Mason jars glistened, packed with peaches and pears. Pint size glass containers would hold his small parts. I'd empty out the wide-mouthed gallon pickle jar, make room for his head. My gut tightened.

Bungee cords stretched in front of the shelves, keeping jars back from the edges. Bungees. No time-consuming knots to slow me down. I would subdue him with bungees, grateful that Father had kept the extras color-coded by size and coiled up on the bottom shelf. They were ready to pack and take along to Brookfield's office.

I sucked at my thumbnail, sore from ripping off duct tape fast in practice last week. Brookfield would be working late as usual this Sunday, alone in his backstore office. I couldn't take the chance someone near the loading docks would hear him, so duct tape was essential. Brushing my fingers across the bristles of my crew cut, I massaged my scalp, counting out fifteen strokes, near the number I'd estimated it would take to sever his arms from his shoulders.

It wasn't as if the superstore hadn't had warnings during construction last year. Those picket lines weren't enough, though. The PriceCuts' protestors should have caused more uproar, thrown themselves in front of the bulldozers, shown it was a matter of life and death.

PriceCuts. Chopping up Mom-and-Pop markets. Like a cancer, choking off a few parts at a time. Turn around one day, and every last independent business will be good as dead. Got to stop it.

Every cell in my body flared with rage, burning hotter now than back on the day we had to close up shop. I walked toward the workbench cupboard to pour some plum brandy to calm me down, but stopped before I reached the workbench. Had to keep a clear head tonight.

I looked over at the bulletin board, studied the pattern I'd sketched, soothed by its black and white presence. The design itself cooled me down, reassured me of success, with its parallel rows of three parts each: an upper arm, a lower arm, and a twenty-dollar bill. Once it hit the news, this picture would bring our town's small businesses back to life.

I shifted my gaze to the chair in the corner, made of branches cut from the gnarly old plum tree out back. A shadowy figure hovered in that dim space. I blinked to clear my eyes. Ever so slightly, Mother nodded approval before her image vanished into the air. I carried her strength, after all.

It was now time to place manager Brookfield into a showcase: display the real man—monstrous at work and monstrous at home. Human Resources Manager. Ha! Thinks he knows what it means to be human. Decent people will be even more put off when they learn of his home life. Setting him out in pieces will get reporters' attention, explode his hush-hush parties into the news. It was good luck when I got invited to that bash of his.

Inviting us staffers to that masquerade last summer showed his arrogance. A combination of July Fourth and a preview of Halloween he called it. Shameless. His wife tramped out in a belly dance costume jingling with coins, blond hair straggling out from under a black wig, directing that guy with the camcorder to tape it when she shook her breasts in the face of the snake handler. Outrageous, both him and that wife, just an aging second-rate actress.

The boa constrictor didn't sway one way or another that night, face-to-face with Belinda while she flaunted her vulgar celebrity, silk pants billowing. Couldn't believe it. She lifted the brown snake and set it around her shoulders, letting the ends trail over her arms like a feather boa I'd seen in pictures of old-time strippers. Like she was daring the snake to put the squeeze on her.

And Steven Brookfield himself—his bright eyes beaming through eye cutouts in his black sequined half-mask—touching and feeling his way around the guests. It was criminal the way he maneuvered Dr. Zasimo's wife away from the crowd. Evil was his middle name—Steven Evil. At home and at work. Time now to expose him and what he represents. I would play into his perversion, use it for good.

Tonight he should be over at the store making up for lost time. The guy didn't actually need to work, just wanted in on the superstore power trip. With their friends from San Francisco, the couple partied out at their estate most Friday and Saturday nights and slept in on Sundays.

It was common knowledge he came in and worked late at PriceCuts Sunday nights to catch up and get ready for Monday morning. That's when he'd interview the needy masses for jobs they were desperate enough to crave. My face still burned with shame thinking about the hoops he put me through, just to get this damn trainee job. After decades of running my own shop.

Spanking clean tools and supplies sat on the workbench, next to my black Nike gym bag: duct tape, razor-edged knives, a sharpener in case the work dulled the steel, large and small plastic bags. I added bungee cords in several lengths and thicknesses and pulled the worn twenty-dollar bills out of my wallet—using rumpled cash would signify money changing hands.

Walking to the bulletin board, I surveyed the collection of advertising flyers stuck there over the years. Mother'd had a hand in making the ones for our shop, but it was dead now. Damn PriceCuts. I pulled off a couple ads I was most proud of. Should leave one or two in his office. Part of my message.

Might be a mistake. Shouldn't let pride trip me up.

Security could be a problem. Management was still uptight over last year's demonstrators and the protests against construction of this first superstore in northern California.

And there were other problems, too. Down in Lodi last summer, that old ice cream vendor and his son Hamid arrested as terrorists. Even the far-off subway bombers in London had added to the tension. I knew PriceCuts was running security cameras out in the front store but it looked like they were too cheap to put them everywhere.

Much as I hated it, applying to work at PriceCuts after Mother died last spring had been a good strategy. Being hired gave me an ID badge, and I knew my way around the backstore offices, loading docks, warehouse spaces and all. I looked over at the old chair in the corner, but it stood empty except for Mother's curly salt and pepper wig, the wig she used going through that damned chemo. Before we lost the shop and our health insurance.

With her wig on, topping my full-length black raincoat, even if the security cameras picked me up, I wouldn't be recognized.

Waggling my fingertips from temples to crown, I gave my scalp another fifteen strokes and stared up through the basement windows at clouds moving in on the moonlit night. Brookfield was in for a midnight special. Got to finish him no later than ten and tie his arms up over his head, so the blood would settle down by three o'clock or so. His head and maybe a couple fingers would be enough to take. Get done by seven Monday morning, slip out the back door of his office through the conference room and leave by way of the busy loading docks.

My plan was sure to kill PriceCuts business—like they'd killed mine.

Here comes a candle to light you to bed,
Here comes a chopper to chop off your head.
—*Anonymous Nursery Rhyme*

TWO

Operation and Outcome

THE FIRST FEW RAINDROPS of fall danced on the windshield during my ten-minute drive. I pulled into the massive parking lot and headed past the storefront windows and signs flashing THINK PRICECUTS! at both sides of the entrance. Think PriceCuts, sure. In the days following this lesson, no one would want to shop here, work here, or ever think that name again.

I cruised past the loading dock and studied the scene. All the guys seemed focused on unloading merchandise from the hulking big rigs, their trailers backed up to the gaping doors of the warehouse wing. I turned into a space where the night crew parked.

Mother's wig sat waiting in the console. I pulled it out, held it to my face and breathed in deep, relishing the faint scent of her, and then stretched it over my scalp. In my full-length black raincoat buttoned up snug, I passed through the front doors of PriceCuts at eleven, an hour before closing, looking like an ordinary customer. Proud of my hidden agenda, I glanced at the bald greeter.

"Take your returns to the last station, Ma'am." He nodded toward my Nike bag.

14

I smiled, not wanting him to hear my voice, and moved as directed but angled off toward the pharmacy aisles. Bending down as if to check out the Epsom salts on a bottom shelf, I pulled off the wig, and stuffed it behind the boxes. Epsom salts didn't move fast. I could get the wig next week on a break.

Standing up, I clipped on my ID badge, keeping my face turned away from the overhead cameras, and made for the rear of the store, my badge jiggling with each step. No problem getting past the customer service desk, staffed by a scrawny kid leaning back in a chair, staring at the ceiling and yakking into his cell phone.

Once into the backstore, I passed the General Manager's door, and then walked by the bench I'd sat on waiting for a job interview last spring. I stood facing the brass plate announcing: "Steven Brookfield, Human Resources Manager." Lucky for me he'd set a tone of familiarity, to say the least, among us staffers. But he was a major player in the gang of greedy-guts. Had to keep my focus on him as a chicken, a deer, a high-class lamb. Anything to dehumanize him so I could do the job necessary.

I unzipped my bag and reached for a hook end of quarter-inch bungee cord, the length of a yardstick. The red and white woven elastic with its dull sheen was sturdy and strong, and I looped the end over my left pinky finger so the hook would be handy.

I knocked on the laminated, pecan-finished door.
"Yeah?"
"Hey, Steven. Like to talk to you."
"Come on in. It's open."

I entered his office and felt myself sink a quarter inch into the sea-green carpet.

"Change your mind about fast-track executive training?" He stood and walked around his cherry-wood desk, hand stretched out in greeting, blue eyes sparkling under his shaggy blond hair. "Thought you might. We need high-energy guys like you. Hope Belinda didn't overdo it at the party?"

I extended my right hand as if to shake his, at the same time I whipped out my left, holding the bungee hook end. Pulling more cord from the bag, I encircled him at the waist, passing the hook into my right hand. I felt like some sort of tailor measuring his waist for a new suit. The odd humor of the scene struck me.

I started laughing. "Yep. That wife of yours. Unbelievable!"

He yanked at the bungee around his middle. "What the fuck!"

"She phoned yesterday and asked me to break in. Wants me to videotape you tied up in your chair, be the lead-in to a film she dreamed up. Says she aims to become a director." As I talked, he tugged at the bungee.

I looked him straight in the eyes. "She wants you to reverse roles, big guy. Play passive for a change. Remember how she loved being cuddled by that boa constrictor?"

Suddenly he shifted into falsetto tones, for God's sake. "You're not here to seduce me, are you big guy?"

"Nah. She just wants to make an X-rated comedy with hubby tied up tight at the office, then switch scenes to show her playing house with her California butler. Corny, but . . ."

I fed out the length of the red plaid bungee and looped it several times around his upper torso, catching his arms in the wrap. He stood wide-eyed and stock-still.

Hooking the two ends together, I finished pinning his arms. "Back up. Sit down in your chair," I ordered.

He nodded. "She's gone bonkers this time." He laughed. "Hurry it up. I've got work to finish, buddy." He backed around the desk, shaking his head, and plunked his big frame into the executive swivel chair. "Okay, sock it to me, Champ." He shut his eyes.

It worked! I made him believe it's some new sex game. I whipped out a longer, thicker bungee and wrapped his legs together, then took two turns around the chair's pedestal base before I hooked the ends, stretching the cord, pinning him tighter.

Grabbing duct tape from my bag, I stood face-to-face with the man who hired me. I pulled out eight inches of the wide gray tape and ripped it clean off.

At the sound of the tape tearing, his eyes flew open. At the same time I plastered it over his mouth and pressed hard at both ends. He began grunting, shaking his head and rocking his torso.

"I'll do the talking now, Mr. PriceCuts." Excited, my voice rose to a high pitch. The plan was working. A surge of pleasure flooded my limbs.

His eyes bulged. He furrowed his blond eyebrows and bobbed his neck, looking like a chicken hawk trying to take flight. I had to get him pinned to the back of the chair and shut up the noisy grunting. Grabbing a short bungee, I twisted it around his head, pulled it past the high back of the chair and stretched it twice around his neck.

His guttural cries faded but his eyes bulged even wider. I'd never witnessed this before on a human. Hell of a note.

I pulled out a white plastic bag from my Nike stash and pulled it over his head. Didn't want to watch as he strangled in his death seat, bucking and twisting. I double checked the door behind his desk, opened it to preview my getaway route through the conference room and out to the loading dock.

After two or three minutes, his grunts faded to silence.

Studying his limp carcass, I smiled with satisfaction and could feel each cell in my body grinning with its own tiny happy face.

I bent to the task, unwound his torso bungees, and lifted both arms above his head, rewrapping them in a prayer position, with an arm bound snug to each ear. Gravity would drain the blood to his lower parts. I needed a clean working environment, not a bloody mess. A neat display meant everything. There would be photos, of course. Not a good idea to set up a bloody mess. I'd always been proud of my work. No loose splintery bones in my shop! A clear-cut message was essential.

Now that his heart no longer circulated blood, a purplish-red color in the legs would announce when the red cells had sunk by gravity through his watery serum. Then I could begin the work I was best at. It wouldn't be that different from cutting up anything else. Just a variation on the shape of the parts.

I busied myself arranging items to underscore the lesson: news photos of anti-PriceCuts demonstrators and "Going Out of Business" sale flyers. But they didn't look all that necessary to the message after all and might give me away. So I stuffed them back into the Nike bag.

Energy for the next stage of the operation pulsed from my heart through my arms to the tips of my fingers. I reviewed my design and how I would position his palms reaching out for the money on his desk blotter. I rehearsed how I'd wrap up a few parts to take from the scene and distribute later in the store if the consuming public and sheep-like employees didn't grasp the lesson.

THREE

Advance Story

CLUTCHING HER PILLOW, Hillary fought back inside the dream.

Stretching down from an inky sky, Charles' finger penetrated through clouds and waggled an inch from her face, keeping time like an accusing metronome. She punched into the damp bundle of goose down, and his image faded away. She shook her head and rubbed open her eyes. Was he really after her or was she running when no one was chasing?

She'd fled New York after collecting the master's degree, hoping to hide away in this corner of California's Central Valley. Give herself time and space to recover from Daddy's death and Charles' disdain. She was worried the advance story she'd been assigned to write might go national. Who could have guessed celebrity designer Jacki Jones would come here to unveil her high tech home improvement system? The story could draw Charles' attention to her byline and provoke his punishing reaction, even kill her career.

Sitting on the edge of the bed, she pushed her fingers through her hair, lifting it off her sweaty scalp, and stared out the bare windows. Pink light spread over the sky and poked through gnarly walnut branches, forming dappled shadows along the white walls of her cottage. She wondered if she'd dug herself a grave by renting here in the dark quiet of Morada's abandoned orchards. It was almost six o'clock. A couple hours until she was to interview the superstore manager about Jacki Jones coming visit.

Throwing on brown sweats, she went out to jog in the dim light. She ran past country houses and shacks, built at random before zoning laws came to this three-square-mile patch of northern San Joaquin County. Soon she slowed to a fast walk. Neither pace was easy since her five foot, eight inch frame now carried over a hundred and eighty pounds. She wanted the jogging to get her back in shape, help her move past feeling weak and abandoned. Back home, after a shower and a quick meal of scrambled eggs and toast along with French Roast coffee, she prepared for the morning's interview at the superstore, hoping the story would be of regional interest only.

Brushing GingerBrown on her eyelashes and blinking fast, she was thankful for the waterproof cosmetic's protection against the evidence of tears. In the past she'd craved her byline on the front page, the way her father used to crave Jack Daniels and belt it down. Said it was part of working his contacts as a newsman covering politics up in Sacramento. His deadly heart attack last May left her feeling like a 35-year-old orphan, needing to cover up her grief. She dragged the bristle brush through her hair hard enough to make it hurt and willed herself not to cry.

After stroking on tawny lip-gloss, she struggled into her extra-large navy blazer. Got to go on a diet—at least she'd started taking her coffee black. She poured the rest of the French Roast into a car cup, grabbed her tote bag and a couple biscotti, and locked the cottage door. Her brand new VW Golf, bought last week with cash from Daddy's insurance, waited in the gravel driveway—trustworthy and solid as his presence. Sliding into its gray leather seat, she felt hugged. Under the canopy of ancient walnut trees, she backed down the driveway, and drove out through the cool October air, her radio tuned to classic rock.

Creedence Clearwater Revival wailed out the song about being stuck in Lodi again. She smiled at the lyric's connections to her life as she sped along Highway 99 past Lodi and headed north toward the superstore. These small towns, mere specks on the map, dotted the old highway between Stockton and Sacramento. The twangy music's image of laid-back Lodi and the region was reassuring. She needed no story going nationwide to stimulate Charles, her snarky ex-boyfriend still back in New York. He might follow through on his threat to make public the secret that could ruin her career.

She scraped her teeth across the chocolate coating of a biscotti. Faded brown vineyards flowed by on both sides of the highway, a testament to the slow reality of the vast farmlands. After the rough year earning her master's in Journalism at Columbia, struggling with double-dealing Charles, and ending with the shock of Daddy's fatal heart attack, she wanted to lie low here, tucked away from urban hustle-bustle. She felt safe in the flatland of this valley, sprawled out like a dusty pancake.

The last bite of crunchy biscotti melted away in her mouth. Taking the off ramp, she steered in the direction of PriceCuts, the huge retail outlet built on plowed-under pastureland last year. It dwarfed the community college temporary buildings next door. Both college and retailer were banking on an upswell in population from the inland housing developments sprouting up in this hot 2005 economy.

PriceCuts' boxy shape loomed ahead, its massive exterior marked by contrasting colors every thirty or forty feet to produce the impression of a row of independent shops. She swung around to the rear parking lot, twenty minutes early for her eight o'clock appointment with the Human Resources manager, pulled into a space, turned off the engine and reviewed her notes. Before slipping out of the Golf's leather embrace, she pinched biscotti crumbs off her navy blazer and popped them into her mouth, looking for chocolate bits but finding none.

She walked towards the back of the massive retail structure. Several PriceCuts semi-trailer trucks unloaded merchandise of all sorts onto docks at the left. Her editor had explained the security setup to get into the backstore for the interview. She stepped up to an open alcove and stood in line behind a man about her height, wearing a black baseball cap. He was being questioned by a young security guard seated at a table.

While she waited, she studied the wall beside the guard, hung with poster-sized photos of demonstrators holding signs protesting PriceCuts gigantic store under construction last year. One carried an oversized placard sporting a hand-drawn axe next to red words stacked up like poetry:

> PriceCuts
> Chops up
> Mom & Pop
> Shops!

The guard glanced at the man ahead of her, then over to the posters, as if to confirm the man's face was not on what looked like a wall of Wanted posters. It was enough to make a person feel on the guilty side, she thought.

The man spoke in a muted voice to the guard and held out a slip of paper. Workers lined up behind her, for the eight o'clock store opening. She always showed up ahead of schedule, like her father trained her. Get there early, leave early, get a scoop story. The guard punched a number into his phone then muttered a few words while the man shifted from one leg to the other, stamping each black Chukka down hard in turn, leaving a faint outline of his footprints on the concrete.

"Okay, go on in." The guard waved toward a narrow door at the right. The man adjusted his cap and scurried into the back of the superstore.

Hillary gave a friendly grin and dragged her fingers through her hair. "Broome," she said. "Hillary Broome. I'm here to interview the HR manager." Angry faces of demonstrators glared from the posters beside his desk. Her heart pounded as if she'd been accused of a crime. "It's with Mr. Brookfield. My editor set it up." She showed him her press card.

"Broome, yeah." He didn't even look at the posters, just checked her name off a list and waved her toward the back door, into spaces the public rarely saw.

Once inside, she pulled her reporter's notebook from her tote, turned to a fresh page and jotted down her impression of the security setup and then the sheet rocked passageway, its rough walls marked off with closed doors. Behind a desk halfway down the hall sat an African-American woman wearing a snug purple jumpsuit.

"I have an appointment with Mr. Brookfield." Hillary smiled at the woman, who looked about the same plus-size as herself. The woman, whose lanyard tag identified her as Clarice Gale, stood and led Hillary a few steps further along the hall.

"Here, honey," Clarice said, waving purple nails in the direction of a stone bench set beside a fake olive tree in a terra cotta pot. "I'll let him know you've arrived."

Hillary thanked her and jotted down her name and description. Appreciating your contacts was rule number one, her father had insisted—get the spelling right on their names. The woman clattered back to her desk in pointy-toe sling pumps, lifted the phone and punched in a number with the tip of a nail. After a few seconds, she punched in more numbers. Then her voice could be heard over a loudspeaker paging Mr. Brookfield.

Hillary waited on the rough bench, edgy but ready, poised with notebook and pencil—the sort her father used, fat and black, the kind she loved ever since he taught her to print, the year before kindergarten.

Ten or fifteen seconds later, the guard from the back alcove arrived to pound on the door. "Mr. Brookfield? Mr. Brookfield?" He banged louder and listened. No sound. He waggled the knob, but found it locked.

He looked at Clarice, who'd followed him to the door. "His Caddy was out in the lot," she said with a frown.

Hillary scribbled notes, flipping the spiral bound pages, adrenaline flowing at their confusion. *Should have brought the camera.*

The guard beat on the door. There was no response. He looked at Clarice. She nodded. He uncoiled a ring of keys from his belt, unlocked the office door and edged it open. Hillary craned her neck and tried to see past him.

One quick peek, and he pulled the door shut. "Call the sheriff!" he hissed at Clarice, now wide-eyed and turning towards her desk. "Tell them come around back!" He punched numbers into his cell phone as he ran down the hall.

Hillary felt invisible in the urgency of their actions. After noting the time, she stepped over and wiggled Brookfield's doorknob. It turned in her hand. Her heart hammered against her stomach. She pushed the door open and stepped inside.

Bare white arms in separate pieces lay on top of the executive desk. She gasped, clenching her notepad and pencil tight to her chest. The bloodless flesh was set out in rows. Cash money lay lined up near the severed limbs. She felt stabbed in the gut at the sight of the black desk blotter and its grisly display. But even worse was what sat behind the desk.

FOUR

Interviews

HILLARY'S EYES DARTED back and forth from the horror on the desk to the headless torso seated behind the desk. She stood frozen a few seconds, then turned back to the open office door. A tall thin man in a tan suit thrust his badge under her nose and introduced himself as Detective Ed Kiffin. She stared at him, struck by the color of his eyes, a jade green.

"Need to talk to you." He jerked his head indicating she should precede him out the door. She felt limp, not sure if she could walk. He took her elbow and led her toward the store's retail floor. As they moved, her hands shifted and begin writing as if with a mind of their own. She jotted down the detective's name and his description as they traveled down the hall. The biscotti lay like a rock in her stomach making its presence known. She swallowed hard a couple times. This must have been what it was like for Daddy at the F Street Boarding House when he was sent to cover the story of them digging up all those bodies years ago. That Sacramento landlady killing for the old men's Social Security checks. Sickening.

She was annoyed by the detective's pressure on her shoulder steering her down the hall but too busy writing to shake him off. Some other man in a suit, portly as Alfred Hitchcock, already had Clarice walking in the same direction, her high heels clacking on the concrete, resounding over voices from law officers crowding into the back of the store.

"Lordy! It's past opening time," Clarice said, looking to her left as they walked by an archway framing a view of the cavernous shopping floor. Far away, customers clustered up against the front store windows, looking like ants along a spill of syrup.

At an open door under a sign announcing "Accounting," the four of them veered off to the right. Someone had started coffee and opened up a pink box of PriceCuts Donuts. The smell of the greasy sweets nauseated Hillary.

The portly man, evidently Kiffin's sidekick detective, steered Clarice toward the coffee set-up. The long room held half a dozen desks, each one tidier than the next, as if the office staff were in some kind of neat-freak competition.

The sight of the deep-fried donuts, added to Hillary's glimpse of the carnage in the manager's office, made her saliva run as if she were going to get sick. That biscotti was definitely trying to come back up. She swallowed two or three times, clamped one hand to her chest and the other to her stomach, and walked to the far end of the room, away from the pink box spotted with grease and in the direction of a chair the lean detective was gesturing toward.

He plunked himself down at the gray desk. Flipping open a small spiral notepad, squinting and leaning his long thin face toward her, he launched into a standard interrogation like on TV. After writing down her name and address, he frowned as she set her notebook and pencil on the desktop as well, explaining she was a reporter and would be taking notes for the weekly *Acorn*. She scribbled a description of the room they sat in.

"How long were you there, at Brookfield's door?" His pen scalloped along the edge of the spiral wires at the top of his blank page while he waited for her reply.

He looks like a bloodhound with that long face. A living cliché. A green-eyed bloodhound. She swallowed, feeling numb. "Three minutes, five at the most."

"How many times have you been to Brookfield's office?"

"Never. Never before." Did he think she was involved in the killing? Her stomach lurched, and she held her lips closed.

"Who did you see nearby?"

"The security guard then the receptionist woman." She nodded in Clarice's direction. "That's all."

He glared at her. "Was there anyone else?"

Wasn't there someone in line ahead of me? She felt on fire from his questions, forced to reveal herself, as if back in the student newspaper classroom with Charles that last day of finals at Columbia.

"What did you see when you got a look through the door?" He jackhammered the point of his pen against the surface of his pad while he waited for her answer.

She wasn't used to being on this side of the questions. She should be asking him, but a lethargy came over her, a whisper took over her voice. "Well, mostly white arms, laid out in a design . . . it looked like, on the desk blotter."

While he scribbled, she wrinkled her nose, sucked in her lips, and rubbed her left hand back and forth across her stomach. She sat silent, crosshatching lines on her notebook into tic tack toes, and then starting to sketch the patterns of the arms on the desk. *It was four pieces, wasn't it?*

The detective flipped to a new page. His eyes bored into her, asking for more, and jumped-started her memory. Her mouth felt dry. She craved fresh lip-gloss but couldn't break away from this oddest of interviews to get some from her tote.

"Four parts, maybe set out like two equal signs." She showed him the design she'd drawn.

He sketched the pattern onto his notepad and nodded. "What else?"

She rubbed her throat. "He was just sitting there, shirtless, facing forward except . . ." She cleared her throat, trying to stop the nausea rising. "Except, he had no head. He was armless. He . . ." She coughed. "He looked like some kind of Greek statue, like a ruin."

Stunned at what her reporter's eye had absorbed in a few seconds, she stared at his fingers racing across the tiny pages of his pad. She waited for him to stop writing and look up before she carried on. "Lying on the desk. Arms." She could barely get the words out, compulsively scratching more sets of parallel lines onto her notebook. "Arms. It looked like too many arms, lined up, you know."

She pressed her dry lips together, craving gloss. "Not natural, cut off, the elbows, not connected . . ." She could hear herself at a distance, babbling, and wondered if he noticed how low and gravelly her voice was.

"That was the first time you ever laid eyes on him?" The detective clicked shut his pen and placed it into his jacket. He reached into an inside pocket, but brought out nothing.

"Well, parts of him." Her stomach was churning. *Detectives can dig secrets out of people.*

He tossed his head in the direction of the coffee and pastries. "Can I get you some?"

She shook her head, and he got up to pour himself a cup of black brew and bring it back to the table. *Thank God he's not a donut guy.*

She stared at Clarice down at the other end of the room, stuck with the fat partner who was chomping on a glazed apple fritter. *Wish I hadn't eaten that biscotti.* Nauseated, she looked down and noticed a paper clip on the floor but resisted the urge to pick it up, had to avoid bending over and disturbing her queasy stomach.

The detective blew on the hot liquid, sipped at it, grimaced, and set it down. He pulled out his pen and continued. "Why were you there? How did you get the interview with him?" He scribbled into his notepad, turning pages as she talked. "Sent by your editor? Name?"

"Roger. Roger Ingram. *The Acorn*, used to be *The Clarion News* before Roger took it over. He doesn't have much other staff besides stringers. I lived in New York for a couple years, near Jacki Jones headquarters. PriceCuts plans to handle the new Jacki Jones Line, you know, JJL?" *Detectives ask more questions than reporters.*

It hit her that she hadn't called Roger yet to report the story, but she couldn't gather the energy to search for her cell phone somewhere down at the bottom of her tote.

The detective began setting down his pen and reaching into his breast pocket every couple minutes, as if searching for a different pen. There was something inept about the man, despite his brusque exterior. She began to consider him as cute but incompetent and wondered why. She wanted to think of anything to help her block out the grisly image of what was left of the HR manager.

"Did you see anyone entering or leaving his office? Did the door move? Did you hear anything? Smell anything?" He kept up his grill, but began tapping his pen on the edge of the table, instead of writing down her responses.

He turned toward his hefty partner in the other corner of the rectangular room. The balding detective had let the receptionist go and studied his own notes as he munched on a maple bar.

"Hey, Walt, you didn't stash away any of those little cigarillos?"

"Nah, you said you're quitting this time for sure." Walt lifted his pastry and chomped down, forcing custard to swell out from the sides. He seemed to swallow the bite whole and able to carry right on talking. "Why don't you get a nicotine patch?"

The detective turned back to Hillary "Okay, young lady."

Jeez. Sounds like Daddy, but he's not that old.

"We're done for now, but don't go far." He took out a business card and scrawled a number next to the San Joaquin County Sheriff information printed on it, then handed it over with a frown. "Here's my cell number if you think of anything you forgot."

He reminded her of the scarecrow in The Wizard of Oz, kind of appealing in a gaunt, driven sort of way. *Cops are in it for power—don't get involved.* Ever since high school, she'd been drawn to the wrong men—always with hazel eyes in various shades— most recent case in point being falling for Charles in

New York when he was just out to suck up to Daddy and his *L.A. Chronicle* contacts.

She'd sworn off men since moving back to California. Detectives, whose job it was to ferret out criminals of all kinds, felt especially dangerous now that she was trying to keep a low profile.

FIVE

A Discovery

HILLARY LEFT THE ACCOUNTING OFFICE and passed the Customer Service section, crowded with workers who'd been herded together waiting to be questioned. She retraced her steps down the corridor toward the rear parking lot, brushing past crime scene investigators. Officers had finished cordoning off the security alcove she'd stepped up to, not more than an hour ago. Media vans had started to congregate and technicians were setting up satellite dishes. She pushed her way silently through reporters throwing questions at her, grateful she'd parked some distance away from the back entrance to the store.

Back in the snug leather cocoon of her Golf, she pulled out her cell phone and reported in to Roger. He was vexed that she hadn't phoned in sooner and that she'd not taken a camera along. He'd already started a news story and was ready for her to fill him in on the details, but he was super eager for her to get her exclusive first-person story up onto their new *Acorn* website.

She wanted to get going, get her scoop story started down at the office, but felt suddenly debilitated, like her blood was chilling down to a sort of solid in her veins. Her hand felt limp, unable to lift her keys to the ignition. She sat there, focused on the wider context of what she'd witnessed. Who could have done this? Why? She'd heard the rumbles. Could this be some kind of retaliation for

PriceCuts' position on wages and health benefits for their employees?

The scene came rushing back into her mind's eye. The image of dismembered arms set out on that huge desk, parallel, like big equal signs, as if placed in a deliberate design. The visual felt like a punch in the gut. It looked like some demented I Ching pattern. What could it mean? Details crowded into her mind's eye. A wedding ring on a finger. Wait a minute—fingers missing? A dollar bill? Saliva poured into her mouth, making her swallow again and again. *Can't throw up here.*

Teeth clenched, hand clamped over her lips, she pushed her way back through the gathering media to the alcove, ducked under the yellow tape to the security desk, grunted at the guard, and waved her press card at him.

"Sorry, lady. Crime scene protocol."

"Sick to stomach," she muttered, taking deep breaths.

"No can do."

She turned her head toward the concrete floor beneath his white laminate table. Her belly began bucking as she tried to hold down the biscotti and coffee while the guard stared, stern-faced. As her heaving intensified, he looked for permission from the officer at the door, and they both waved her into the store.

Rushing back to the reception station, she found Clarice at her post, coolly directing police and coroner's staff and turning back media types who'd slipped in.

Hillary tried to get her attention, talking through clenched teeth to keep herself from throwing up.

"Bashroom?" She spoke from under white tissues she'd grabbed off Clarice's desk. "Shick."

"It's just past Mr. Brookfield's office but that's jammed with cops, honey. Here." She swiveled around to push a panel on the wall behind her desk, revealing a darkness beyond. Reaching around to snap on some lights, Clarice waved Hillary into a room. "Back to the left rear you'll find the washroom, sugar."

Pursing her lips, Hillary stepped in from the hallway. In a flash, her eyes took in the white-walled perimeter. An oval conference table stretched out down the middle. She hurried for the door with the restroom symbol, rushed in and made it to the toilet before she threw up.

After two or three minutes gasping and hunched over the toilet, she stood to clean up the mess she made, grateful there were plenty of paper towels and that she had managed to keep her clothes unsoiled. She scooped cold water onto her face and smoothed her hair with wet palms, feeling her stomach starting to settle. She wove her hair into one long French braid down the back. *You need to be getting your story out!*

She reentered the bright room, disoriented and wondering how to get back to the hallway and out to the parking lot. Who knew the backstore held such a maze of rooms? Feeling like Alice in Wonderland, uncertain how to get back to Clarice's desk, she flipped a wall switch. A four-foot wide floor-to-ceiling panel slid aside to reveal Brookfield's office from the back side of his desk. She stood paralyzed, holding her breath, eyes locked on to the same bizarre scene she'd glimpsed earlier, except this time from the other side of the desk.

Even back in New York City, gruesome violence this up close and personal hadn't been part of daily life. She knew covering Jacki Jones's enterprise could boost her byline in a dangerous way, but writing stories in places where people got killed and chopped into pieces might get downright deadly. She'd had self-defense in high school and karate in New York, but her skills were not all that strong. Helpless dread flooded her limbs.

She looked around the dead manager's office, unable to avoid focusing on the display of body parts. Those parts were a major aspect of this story and she needed to create a word picture of them. But she felt sick and empty.

The office bulged with crime scene personnel. She spotted a piece of green paper near Brookfield's desk, just before a photographer aimed his camera at the torn item and popped off two successive flashes. Then his partner lifted the green paper with big tweezers and put it into a manila envelope marked "evidence."

The thin detective who'd questioned her was crouched near the dead man's desk, studying the carpet and what might have been faint footprint impressions. Crime specialists worked in the silent office, entirely absorbed.

Hillary forced herself to study the grisly pattern set out on the black desktop blotter like some maniac's sculpture. The wall had opened up like a theater curtain, leaving her framed as a repeat audience to this horror show, a journalist fighting paralysis yet feverish to get her exclusive story uploaded. It was sure to be picked up by the national media—an exhilarating and frightful prospect.

SIX

A Connection

SENSING A SHIFT in the room's air currents, Detective Ed Kiffin looked over his shoulder to discover the woman he'd sent away just ten minutes ago. He straightened up, his knees creaking.

"Hey, lady. We sent you home." The sight of the reporter gave him a quick and welcome break from this horror show. Plump in a shapely way, it flashed through his mind that she looked cuddly.

"I was sick. The receptionist from out there . . ." She jerked her thumb over her shoulder toward the room behind her. ". . . let me in for the bathroom." She stepped toward him. "I'm leaving."

"Not tramping over evidence, you're not," he said, snapping his thoughts back to the crime scene. "Stand still!" *How'd that wall get open?* He turned to look the other way. *Why the hell was giving up little cigars a good idea? Hardly ever lit the damn things with all the laws against them. Got to pick some up from—*

His brief meditation was interrupted by the sight of a muscular young man who came striding through the front office door.

"Hey, Doc Waldo," Ed shouted. "Take a look at our 'parts is parts' guy."

Grim-faced, the Medical Examiner approached the desk and surveyed the neatly laid out upper extremities of what had been Steven Brookfield.

Solving this case could redeem Ed's reputation and more important, his self-confidence. It had been five years since his teenaged daughter had been killed in a hit and run down in Stockton. All this time, and no leads. He felt like a failure ever since.

The crime scene techs moved aside to make room for Doc Waldo to start his preliminary exam. Latex gloved, he rotated Brookfield's naked and headless trunk as it sat, minus arms, in the executive chair. Ed was fascinated by the ME's precision handling dead bodies. Examining the victim, the doctor began his routine, speaking into a portable mic attached to his lapel.

"Unclothed arms disarticulated from the trunk at the shoulders and also at the elbows. Head not in evidence. No gunshots or stab wounds apparent to the unclothed upper trunk. Legs attached, and clothed." He examined and commented on the four naked body parts placed in parallel pairs on the expanse of the black felt blotter. "Upper arms, left and right, lower arms, left and right, hands attached, missing index fingers and pinkies on both hands. No gunshot or stab wounds, no defensive wounds. Except for a plain gold wedding band on the left ring finger and . . ." He stooped down closer to the desk. "A Michael Kors goldtone bracelet watch on the left wrist, all upper limbs stripped of clothing and severed cleanly from the trunk at the shoulders and elbows."

As the ME articulated bit-by-bit an accumulation of data on the murder victim, Ed's mind couldn't help moving toward implications of the cuts. At the same time, he felt a mixture of shame and outrage that this kind of thought process had never turned up his daughter's killer. Five years and all that got resolved was to break up his miserable marriage and move the ex-wife out to New Jersey. She'd taken their other daughter with her. He still wasn't used to living alone but hadn't been up to starting a new life, either. He was aware of the reporter standing framed in the doorway, aware that he liked her redheaded presence, jotting into her notebook.

"Shockingly little blood," Doc Waldo noted. "Any surgeon would be proud." He bent down to lift up the edge of Brookfield's pant leg, first one then the other. "Extreme lividity to the lower limbs."

Breaking Ed's fixation with the examination procedure, a slurry voice with a Southern accent boomed into the office from behind the reporter.

How the hell had this guy gotten in? Behind Mr. Southern Drawl, Ed could see that African-American receptionist standing at a doorway beyond, drawing Ed's attention back to the mystery room revealed a few minutes ago by the reporter's appearance. Looked to be some kind of conference room, maybe.

"Real sorry about this, ya'll." The portly man with a fringe of straight white hair spoke in a loud voice. "Ron Tompkins, General Manager, from the office next door. Sure don't want a ruckus in our nice new store, now do we? Don't want our customers kept outside, hear?" He puffed out his cheeks, looking like a fat white frog.

Ed shifted back into lead detective mode. He pointed past the general manager to Clarice, standing on the other side of the conference room, and glared at the reporter who was jotting notes on her long thin pad. "Mr. Tompkins, and you, young lady, back out toward the receptionist, out that direction and not in through this crime scene." *How the hell do I know that hidden room might not be part of the crime scene, too?*

As Ed pointed the two interlopers toward the reception desk, he unblocked the full view of Brookfield's office for the general manager, revealing the four dismembered segments of his dead colleague laid out atop the desk.

Tompkins let out a low whistle. "Don't this beat all?" He stared at what remained of his fellow manager. A second later, he bent over double and let out an "oof!" as if someone had punched him in the belly. He covered his mouth with a handkerchief and paused a moment. Turning his head to the detective, he muttered, "Tell me you haven't let the press in here."

Ed didn't let on that the woman was a reporter. Couldn't the manager see her scribbling on her notepad? How could management expect to keep this kind of thing out of the news?

"Get them to the interview room." Ed motioned for his partner Walt to steer the manager and the reporter out.

As soon as the conference room—or whatever the hell it was—was empty, Ed directed crime scene tape be stretched across that doorway, too. Ed left Clarice at her desk to monitor the action, keeping the long corridor and offices closed off to all but essential law enforcement.

Jesus H. Christ. Ed patted his pockets, longing for a smoke of any sort. Walt led their return into the long narrow accounting office and seated Ron Tompkins by Ed. With a loud harrumph, Walt plunked himself down at the opposite wall with— what was her name? Ed flipped open his spiral memo pad. Hillary. Hillary Broome. A newsy for *The Acorn.* Odd she would return to the scene. Was it really because she was sick? Walt could take a turn with her. *Reminds me of my ex, when we were young, with that fair skin and hair so much redder than mine.* Ed turned to Tompkins.

The well-upholstered manager, who could have been an older brother to Walt, sat swiping a red and white-checkered handkerchief across his shiny forehead.

"Who would want to hurt Brookfield?" Ed drilled questions into the store manager. "Did he have any enemies? What was your relationship? How long had he worked here?" The manager's head was cocked in the direction of the front of the store. He ignored Ed and flipped open his cell phone to make a call.

In the distance, Ed could hear faint shouts of shoppers escalating into pounding on the plate glass windows next to PriceCuts entrance doors.

"Closed temporary, due to emergency—yeah, post it and pass coupons out." Tompkins snapped shut his cell and turned to glare at Ed. "Damn circus. Got to give out double rain checks for Monday SuperPriceCuts Day. Never know if publicity will help us or hurt us."

"What do you know about Brookfield?" Ed started over on his questions. "Was he in charge of benefits? Who wanted him out of the way? What about his personal life?"

"He was HR, you know, hiring and firing—human resources. Since we expanded last month to carry everything from sofas to soup, his job got tougher. And now, Jacki Jones design system is coming. I was thinking about finding him an assistant." He squirmed in the lightweight office chair.

Ed waited, comfortable alternating a barrage of questions with silence. Most people could not stand quiet for more than a few seconds and would start volunteering information just to fill the empty air.

"He could have been having trouble with his wife," the manager offered. "They held parties out in Morada. Lizzy Jane and I went once, but . . ." He swiped at his forehead with his rumpled handkerchief.

Ed scribbled into his notepad, flipped to a new page, and nodded at him.

"They might have been into things that we . . ." The manager looked around the room.

"We?" The hardest part of the job was waiting through the hemming and hawing. Ed ached for a small cigar to roll around in his fingers, inhale the spicy scent.

"The wife and I, and . . ." Tompkins fell silent and squinty-eyed. He seemed to be listening for something. A faint *wop wop* filtered into the narrow room and grew louder moment by moment.

"And. And what?"

"The company, they don't want us doing shit like that."

"Like what?"

Helicopter blades churned the air overhead, sounding like they could rip right through the roof. Tompkins' shoulders straightened and he turned his full attention to Ed.

"I don't know, kinky maybe. Like that. I don't want to know." He was shouting. "But Steven, he might have been in trouble. Yeah." Tompkins mopped the back of his sweaty pink neck and rolled his shoulders forward then back, popping his joints. "I should have fired him, but he got all his work done, and had a way with people. Know what I mean?"

"Okay. So wife trouble, drugs trouble." Ed waited to see if Tompkins would contradict the notion of drugs. When he didn't, Ed made a note and went on. "What other kinds of issues?"

"We live in this pressure cooker, bias from the liberal press and the union troublemakers. Headquarters will have my ass for this bad publicity. People think we're rich guys who don't care, but it's not like that."

"What's it like?"

"Like being targets, like we're stamped with a bull's eye for any crazy ass fool who wants to take a shot at us. That's what that conference room's really for, our hideaway, getaway. Call it the 'white room.' Should of saved Steven."

"Our team will be going over that room, too. Could be part of the crime scene." Ed closed his note pad and started to slip it into his breast pocket, feeling around once more for a smoke. "Thanks, Mr. Tompkins. Don't get in the way of the investigators but stick around. We'll get back to you." He waved a deputy over to escort the manager out.

Tompkins pulled out his cell phone and punched in a number. "Yeah, land it. Move the guys into the white room." Tompkins flipped shut his phone and left the interview room.

Ed and Walt looked at each other, wordless, and stood to watch the manager hurry down the hall and turn in to his office. Several men in street clothes who'd been huddled in the corridor filed in to Tompkins' office behind him. The last man in banged the door shut.

With Walt in tow, Ed marched down the hall and opened the pecan-paneled door into Tompkins' office to find it empty, with the wall behind open to the white room. The thwapping sounds of chopper blades cut through the air, as the helicopter lifted off the huge superstore's roof and departed to the east.

"Some guys are literally above the law. They're never going to make the big bucks like Wal-Mart, when they spend on equipment like that." Ed frowned at Walt. "We'll have to interview those other guys later."

Ed walked back to the reporter in navy. She sat staring into the pink box of pastries, empty now except for a raised donut with one bite taken out. Walt had questioned her, but Ed figured it wouldn't hurt for him to keep it going.

"Why did you come back?" Part of the work was following up what others might overlook, but some tasks were more enjoyable than others. She was an intriguing blend of self-sufficiency and vulnerability, and had veered him some degrees off his usual all-business approach. He double-checked her left hand. No ring.

The deep tone of her voice had a soothing effect. "My breakfast biscotti wanted to come back up, you know? The guard let me in, to keep his desk clean." She wrinkled her nose, lightly sprinkled with freckles. "I've got to get over to my office, get going on this piece. I'm not a suspect, am I?"

"Maybe a person of interest." Ed smiled. "I'll need to follow up with you later. In your story, write just the general points—no details on how the parts were set out. We need to keep some cards close to the chest."

She nodded. "I have to get to the *Acorn* office, but later I'll be over at the college, next door." She pointed east. "I've got to be on hand," she wrinkled her nose as she said the last word. He nodded.

"I mean be there while the students get the Clearwater College paper ready to go to print. You could finish up your questions then." She looked at him with gray eyes so dark he could barely tell where the iris left off and the pupils began. She gave a faint grin, flashing dimples that framed her lips, glossy and natural looking.

That smile, with the lopsided dimples. Dimples were his weakness—joy and anguish—Mary Beth had them, too, dimples no one would ever see again. He shoved thoughts of his daughter's death out of his mind, like he'd done countless times before.

He raised his eyebrows—awful friendly of her to ask him over to the college. Hillary Broome, right? He flipped back through his notes to double-check her name and address. A reporter on his side might come in handy. He needed all the help he could get.

SEVEN

A Notification

ED SLAPPED A DOME LIGHT onto the unmarked's roof and sped the five miles south down 99, headed to the Morada mansion Steven Brookfield had shared with his bride, Belinda.

Death notification took steely nerves. Ed knew Walt could handle it better than he could, especially in the past five years. They needed to beat the noon news. Belinda probably watched it for the celebrity angles.

The Brookfield estate fence ran nearly a half-mile along the country road. A wrought iron gate prevented vehicles from entering the property, so Ed pulled over to the side, got out and pushed the buzzer fastened to a black iron post.

"Yes?" A cool voice articulated the word over an intercom.

"San Joaquin County Sheriffs. Need to talk to Mrs. Brookfield."

"She's indisposed at the moment."

"We'll wait."

Silence.

Motioning for Walt to listen for the voice to return and let them in, Ed started pacing off the exterior perimeter of the fence, its metal bars partially obscured with ivy. His size thirteens crunched along layers of leaves underfoot. He turned left at the corner, moving away from the road. Ahead, a boxy shape rose a couple feet off the ground. As he got closer, he could see a blowup mattress pushed close to the vine-covered fence.

What the . . . ?

He pulled at the edge of the rubberized surface. One mattress slid off, and a matching one lay beneath. The set resembled a cake with no frosting between the layers. Replacing the top one, he stepped up onto it. From there, he could see over the ivy-covered fence into a two-story wall of windows. What seemed to be a huge living room took up the ground floor. The second floor looked to be a master bedroom. He could see a canopied four-poster. His eyes locked on to a voluptuous blonde that could have been in one of those paintings by Rubens. Must be the widow Brookfield, walking around, naked.

For sure this was a peeping Tom platform. From the condition of the widow, Ed knew he had time to look the place over before she would be dressed and ready for them and their news. He walked toward the rear of the estate, outside the fence line and under the canopy of the surviving walnut trees still standing from Morada's orchard days. When he reached an open field to the right, he stopped. Signs from the San Joaquin County Public Works department warned against proceeding further. The field was set aside for storm drainage. Never hurt to scope out plans to maneuver in case the peeping Tom raised his perverted head later, and he and Walt were forced to chase through this backwater territory.

Returning to the front gate, Ed discovered their car still there but Walt had disappeared. Ed buzzed the intercom.

"Yes?" The voice duplicated its earlier frosty tone.

"Detective Walt Gaines in there?"

"A Sheriff's deputy is waiting in the living room, yes."

"I'm his partner."

"Very good, sir."

The electronically controlled gate swung open and Ed drove the unmarked in, taking his time rolling along the circular driveway to the front door. He parked, stepped out onto a decomposed granite path, and walked over to the right corner of the house. Walt stood looking out from the inside, watching Ed. In response, Ed pointed toward the back of the house and set out to walk the inside fence perimeter. By the time he completed the circuit, rang the front doorbell and was ushered in by the tight-lipped butler, Walt had already started questioning the widow. Must have got the bad news over with. Looked like she was holding it together so far.

"He didn't have any enemies." The well-preserved woman stared at Walt with a vacant look in her violet eyes. "My father warned me I could, could do better, but Steven was so . . ." Reaching into what looked like a black velvet dressing gown, she pulled out a small handkerchief and pressed it to her eyes, dabbing each one several times.

She frowned and turned her gaze to Ed, who offered the standard platitudes. "Sorry for your loss. Appreciate your cooperation. You were saying your husband was so . . ." He let his voice trail off.

"Charming, full of energy. That man defined the word 'charisma.'" She gave the word three distinct syllables, in a joyful tone, punctuated with a wide smile, duplicating the look he'd seen of her on the cover of *The Globe* when he'd been standing in line at Safeway, buying frozen dinners and cigars.

"How was your marriage?" Ed continued while Walt got up and wandered the room, looking out each window.

"We were newlyweds. Married two years ago on Halloween. We love costumes." She paused and drew in a sharp breath. "Loved. Steven bought me this place, played the toy soldier in the black forest and called me his tiny ballerina. You know that song?" He shook his head with no comment, notepad open on his knee.

"Steven wanted to show he could take care of me, and not the other way around." She blotted her eyes, checking the handkerchief for mascara. "He didn't have a jealous bone anywhere, if you know what I mean." She leaned forward, her gown falling away from her firm white breasts, uncaged by lingerie. "Would you like a drink, Detective?" She smiled and dabbed again under her eyes.

"What might he have to be jealous of?" Ed patted his coat pocket out of habit, feeling for a nicotine fix he knew wasn't there.

"Nothing really. We trusted each other. Life should be enjoyed, don't you agree?" She looked at Walt, returning from his tour of the room, and focused on his round form. "I can see you appreciate fine food." She stood and reached out to pat Walt's protruding belly. "How about a snack? Our chef is a wizard."

"No, thanks, Ma'am." Walt took a step back and frowned. "I'm sorry to have to ask this, but were you or your husband having an affair?"

"Affair? Affair?" She pursed her lips into a pout. "We both had special friends if that's what you mean, but we wouldn't hurt each other with an affair of the heart. We threw the best parties—

what's life without some fun? Steven was a great host. Everyone loved him, men and women both."

"Can we get a list of your guests?"

"Henry, get the detectives a copy of our invitation list, please." She motioned to the tall, slim man standing ramrod stiff at the doorway, who nodded once and disappeared.

"Are we done? I need to get myself together, gentlemen. I have a wake to plan—Steven would want us to party big time to remember him. We can celebrate what would have been our second anniversary at the same time." The blonde stood, rewrapped her dressing gown, and moved in the direction of the entry. "Call if you have any more questions, please. And you're welcome to come to Steven's party. Don't feel shy."

"Yes, Ma'am." They spoke in unison.

"One thing. Call me Belinda, not Ma'am—that makes a woman feel old, don't you know?" She flashed a brilliant smile then handed the detectives off to her butler, who motioned toward the front door with some white papers in hand, the list of Brookfield party invitees. She ascended the wide, circular staircase, pausing midway to gaze down. "Don't be strangers, now. Hear?"

* * *

Once outside the gate, Ed led the way down the road and turned left to go back alongside the fence line. He pointed out the double-stacked mattresses to Walt. "I think a wannabe partier had a private station here. Take a look at his perch. Let's get some lab guys out to check it over."

They moved along the fence line and spotted a video camera fastened to an oak tree growing inside the fence, aimed at the mattress on the ground. "You think the newlyweds could have been in on the peeping?" Walt asked.

"Looks like they might have had a different way of being married," Ed said. "We'll have to get CSIs to take down that camera and ask wifey if there are other tapes, too."

"Watching those could be like renting adult movies." Walt wiped his sweaty forehead and frowned.

"Sounds like she'll cooperate, might even want to show off. She wouldn't have put out a hit on her husband for the publicity, would she?" This case might land the county more media attention than those Lodi terrorists last summer.

Walt shook his head. "Stranger stuff has happened."

"I'll give her a call when I get a minute. Warn her of possible peeping Toms and see how she takes it." Ed got into the car. "You know that redheaded reporter, we talked to her twice in the store this morning?"

Walt nodded, grinning. "Yep."

"Name of Hillary Broome. Told her I'd go by the college where she works, later on today. Follow up, you know? Said she lives out here in Morada. Need to warn her, too, on a possible peeper."

Walt looked at him through narrowed eyes. "Sniffing out some heat in the forest, are you?"

Ed ignored his partner of the past ten years, who'd witnessed the anguish of his divorce, on top of the hit and run of Mary Beth. He flipped through his notes for Hillary's address before he turned on the ignition, gunned the engine in place, and made a U-turn, back to the offshoot road her cottage was on. Wouldn't hurt to know where she lived.

EIGHT

An Exclusive

HILLARY RUSHED OVER to the *Acorn* office and parked on the street, behind Roger's white Mustang. It was nearly noon.

Roger sat at his computer, scrolling through the Associated Press website. He glanced up over his glasses then back to the screen. The story must not have hit yet. She rushed past Mildred at the customer counter and slammed her tote bag onto her desk. After digging out her notebook, she opened a new file and called out at him, using the nickname from their college days on the student newspaper. "Hey, Doc, where's your boilerplate on the cut-up body?"

"In your email, Dopey." He scraped his desk chair back against the rough wood floor with a loud squawk. She winced and wished he'd invest in some chair sliders. She opened his email attachment, saved it to her drive, and scanned the sentences he'd written based on her phone call from the store.

He planted his lanky frame next to her, looking over her shoulder. She glanced up at his calm face, his lips puckered in that way he held them. Listening. You had to be a good listener. That was his main emphasis to her journalism students when he visited as a guest speaker over at the college.

She felt jolted and jazzed as if she'd jumped out of an airplane, skydiving, so much so that her usual anxiety over being observed when writing was at a low ebb. "Got to spice this up," she said. "Right down the road, over at PriceCuts. Not just a kill, but severed body parts, scattered all over a desktop. Looked like some kind of pattern, message."

He nodded.

Her mind sped faster than on that final deadline day at Columbia. She plowed her fingers through her hair and sucked in the dusty air of the old office. Sunbeams poured through the front window, lettered with a gold sign proclaiming the *Clarion News* the oldest newspaper in San Joaquin County. Roger had inherited the struggling weekly from his grandfather, renamed it, and invited Hillary to help him bring it into the twenty-first century with a web presence. He hadn't had the window repainted with the new name yet.

"Want to run it straight news or a first-person feature from my view as a witness?" Hillary looked at him, eager to get flying with her ninety-plus words per minute.

"Go ahead with the straight piece first." Roger frowned and pursed his lips. He stuck his thumbs in the pockets of his unbuttoned vest, his fingers bracketing his bronze belt buckle announcing in all-caps to anyone bold enough to bend down and read it: NEWSMAN—Truth, Justice, and the American Way. She loved his old-time demeanor, so like her father's.

Roger hadn't frowned when she'd updated him on the story of her problem, just about the worst thing a writer could do. Years ago at Sac State when they worked on the student paper, The Hornet, there was a case of a mother abusing her child until the five-year-old died. Covering the tragedy threw Hillary into an altered state, anguished over her own mother running out on her and her father. To finish the story before deadline, she lifted a line from a *Sacramento Bee* piece on the crime.

Ever since, she feared the compulsion to plagiarize might hit her at any time, but especially if a mother was involved. Who could have guessed she would have been assigned a story on the mothers of terrorists for her final exam at Columbia. The "P problem" she called it. Roger she could trust with her shameful breach of ethics, but not Charles, her snarky editor and boyfriend at Columbia. He had betrayed her with another woman—would he unmask her secret, too? She was grateful for her new @acorn.com email address and prayed he would let the past go, leave her alone.

Hillary's insides quivered. No mothers in this PriceCuts dismemberment—yet anyway. She wanted to get this story up on the new website she'd created for the *Acorn*, but an icy fear slowed her at the same time. What if the story went national and irked Charles? He could spill the beans if her byline eclipsed his.

The five W's of journalism jiggled their usual dance. Who, what, where, when, why—and that essential straggler, how? The victim she knew, the crime, the location, the date. Get it all onto the screen. For now, ignore the *why* and *how*.

She forced herself to type, trying to get the pieces to come together like the letters of a word. She felt like a child in the days before computers, watching her father down at his *L.A. Chronicle* office across from the Capitol. He would pound his Olympia typewriter in a two-finger style, frowning in concentration, under the pressure of a deadline. Pressure, always pressure.

They had felt his energy at home, too, like a physical force. It energized Hillary but wore down Mother, who yearned for recognition as an artist. After his Pulitzer, won as part of a team covering an airline disaster, Mother could no longer tolerate his success. All the fuss was more than she could take. She left them when Hillary was ten. Ran off with her art teacher to some island in the Pacific.

Hillary yanked herself back to the present. Okay, deadline pressure's simply a form of energy, she chided herself. Use it. You deserve this story. You were the first to see in that door, spot those dead white arms laid out like that. How to create a word picture? She flipped through the doodles she'd drawn at the store but tossed the notebook aside.

Think. Think. Sketch out the patterns. Get into the scene.

The layout was too big to draw on the back of the outdated press releases she generally used for scratch paper. "We have any old newsprint?" She stared at Roger, the ever-patient one. He nodded toward the back of the newsroom, at a table the *Clarion News* folks used to work at before computer layout was common. Blank newsprint sheets still lay on top of the table, only partially covered with old press releases. *Good thing Roger never wants to throw anything away.*

She stood and grabbed a fat black pencil—every time she held one, she thought of her father keeping them sharp and ready. She muttered as she sketched. *Should have drawn the design better then.* The shock of the scene had frozen her in place. How were the arms laid out on the desk? Kind of like pictures of I Ching sticks maybe? What did those funny patterns with lines in rows mean? She'd seen them on posters years ago, along with yin yang circles.

Roger stood nearby, pulling at the front edges of his brown corduroy vest. His steady gaze calmed her, same as when she'd come home from New York in shame last May. She'd felt safe enough to tell him the truth about her problem, get him to agree to help her guard against temptation. She treasured their friendship. With a gay buddy, she didn't have to worry about any romantic relationship issues.

Her right hand swayed back and forth like the needle on a seismometer when an earthquake is in progress, drawing lines across the pale face of the newsprint. "Three on this side, parallel," she said. "And three on the other side. Three sets of two. They were laid out on purpose, Doc. Must have been."

He clasped his hands and rested his chin on them, elbows propped on the old light table. He watched as she rambled and scratched at the paper with the soft black pencil.

"Or was it two sets of three? It wasn't just arms though." She shot Roger a look. "Laid out on a dark gray or maybe black desk blotter, like yours. Some money, something green?"

Suddenly she remembered the detective's warning not to make public details about the design, and a calm fell over her. She went back to her desk. "What angle on the story did you say you wanted?"

"Take it straight news," Roger said, "until we find out what's what. Type it up and shoot it over to me. Forget describing the layout of the arms for now. Didn't the detectives tell you to skip details only the killer would know?"

"Just what I was thinking," she said, her fingers flying across the keys.

* * *

Within a half hour, they got the story up on *The Acorn* webpage, ignoring her first-person account for now, beating other news outlets, and ready for the next morning's print edition. She felt like collapsing, but had to go over to the college, sit with the students on deadline putting the school paper to bed.

Roger said he would write the obit on Brookfield tomorrow. She told him she'd go with him out to interview the widow if he would cook for her at the cottage tonight. He agreed to go make his Linguine Pesto, and she double-checked that he had a spare key to the cottage in case he got there before her. The cottage belonged to his retired aunt, who rented it out to go on a world cruise that seemed to be stretching out into years of living at sea, making friends in every port.

* * *

Hillary felt satisfied, holding herself together after what she'd witnessed, and getting out that scoop of a story. While she was away at Columbia, California's Central Valley had been in the news. In the perverse way of journalists hungry for bylines, she felt proud the area was hitting the bigs with the Christmas tragedy of pregnant Laci Peterson's disappearance from her Modesto home and then last year, the Lodi father and son terrorist investigations.

She wanted to make a name for herself, but at the same time the truth about her problem would be better kept buried. Now that it looked like media were converging to cover this gruesome crime, she might be competing with the likes of CNN and the networks.

East Coast newspapers might not even cover it though. Charles and his pals at Columbia wouldn't follow news from a small burg like this. But worry over his ruining her reputation hovered in her mind, and she never checked her email without feeling on guard.

She drove up to Clearwater College. She'd included mystery thrillers on her extra credit list because she wanted her journalism students to learn to build tension into their writing. This PriceCuts crime story was thrilling like fiction could never be. Moving back to California might have been a good idea, after all. *There's no reason Charles or any of them should be looking for stories by Hillary Broome.*

NINE

An Observation

FORTIFIED BY A STOP at McDonald's, Ed and Walt returned to PriceCuts' accounting office in the backstore. Ed nodded at his protégé Laurel Mendoza, taking statements from mid-level managers, independent contractors, and other workers who'd shown up at the back entrance that morning, ready for an ordinary Monday. Ed had ordered the guards to bring them in for questioning. He felt lucky to get so many of them coming here rather than have to call them in to the small sheriff's outpost in Clearwater.

The gorgeous Mendoza and her burly black partner, both recently promoted from patrol, worked the interviews. Ed and Walt regrouped in a corner, wondering if they would have to call in the FBI and which of them would give a statement to the media. All the while they eavesdropped on their rookies, who were now interviewing a man in his early sixties named John Stoney, according to the ID hanging from his PriceCuts' lanyard.

"Brookfield hired people forced to work here as an alternative to starving. What kind of life is that?" The wiry man with a gray crew cut seemed eager to talk. "He was like the auctioneer when plantation owners bought and sold slaves, you ask me. Brookfield kept up a front but, hell, it would kill me to do that kind of work."

"Why's that, Mr. Stoney?" Mendoza gazed at him with her blue-green eyes, her open face an invitation for truth to spill out, while her partner scowled steadily as he paced a small circular path nearby, their way of playing good cop/bad cop.

"I was forced here, myself." Stoney pulled at his sparse sideburns, a dark salt and pepper. "Fifty years of running Stoney's Market flushed down the toilet when this giant outfit comes in and . . ." His voice faded away.

"And what?" Mendoza hadn't learned yet to leave a silence for the poor devils to talk into. Ed made a mental note to work with her on that.

"Nothing. Wife says I'm lucky to have a job. Meat manager trainee, at my age." The corners of his mouth sagged. "Are we done?" He stood and turned to go.

"We may need to get back to you. Who in the meat department might have had something against Brookfield?" She kept up her line of questioning.

"We were all beholden to him but no one liked him. None of the working stiffs will be sorry he's dead, though it gives us a bad name to see a man killed and cut up like a chicken."

Ed was surprised the details had leaked out already.

"That's the way a chicken's slaughtered," Mendoza's brawny partner broke in with a growl. "Back on her patch of land between Lodi and Galt, my grandmother used to swing the birds around in the air and stab 'em with an ice pick. Drain the blood herself and cut up the chicken nice and neat right at the joints."

"Yeah," Stoney said. "That's how it's done, all right. Folks who grew up on real ranches know how to take apart a bird. The way poultry comes in at PriceCuts, blocks of frozen meat, it's not the same." He shook his head. "We're lucky we get to cut up anything, with the prepackaged stuff starting to take over." Jaw clenched, the old manager trainee trudged out toward backstore warehouse of the huge retail space, still empty of customers while crime lab investigators worked the scene.

As the hours passed, Ed kept tabs on the other sheriff's staff they'd called in to work a sort of assembly line. Seemed that about half the middle managers resented Brookfield and half didn't. Same with clerks and greeters, who'd arrived for work at the back door to start their part-time shifts, not having heard the news.

On the other hand, independent operators who ran small shops lining the inside walls of PriceCuts said they liked Steven Brookfield. Every one of them claimed to have respected the now-dead manager except Dr. Zasimo. Ed stood nearby as Mendoza interviewed Zasimo, the chief optometrist from the Spec-tacular Eyes alcove up near the front of the store.

"Brookfield? On the outside, a good man," said the doctor in a low voice, with the faintest of Middle Eastern accents.

"Real friendly. More than friendly." The optometrist slid the point of a pale orange toothpick into the space between his two front teeth and waggled it around. It reminded Ed of the little cigar no longer clenched in his jaw, and he resisted the urge to pat his empty breast pocket.

Mendoza asked what Zasimo meant. Her partner reached inside his pants pocket, pulled out and unwrapped a piece of Wintermint gum.

"Not that I approve, but I understand when a man outside the faith is attracted to my wife . . ." The doctor squinted his eyes, looking away from

Mendoza's gaze, and watched her partner fold the gum into his mouth and start chewing.

"Did Brookfield make advances to her?" Mendoza leaned across the neat desk, closer to the white-coated, middle-aged man.

Ed's sixth sense prickled, and he made a show of being engrossed in paperwork nearby.

"Once, but that was enough. I got that picture fast." The doctor took off his rimless glasses, set them on the desk, and rubbed his eyes with his fists. "Yes. Once. Out at their house, you know, out in Morada in all the trees. You have been there?"

"When was this?" Mendoza glanced at her notebook. "What date, if you remember?"

"Fourth of July, this past summer. They called it a freedom theme but it was not the kind of freedom I came over to America for." He put his glasses back on and blinked three or four times.

"What happened?"

"While some synchronized swimmers put on a show in the pool, he disappeared with my Hayaam." He repositioned his toothpick with a stabbing motion.

"Where did they go?"

"I was distracted." He took out the cedar toothpick and broke it in half. "She wouldn't tell me anything. Said she didn't want trouble for me at work." He threw the toothpick halves into a black metal wastebasket.

"So, why do you think someone might want Brookfield dead, Dr. Zasimo?"

"Why should that kind of unbeliever live?" The doctor stood. "May I go?"

"Sure, but don't leave town. We may need to get back to you." Mendoza handed him her card.

By late afternoon, the investigators had identified Stoney, Zasimo, and several other employees as persons of interest. Ed wanted to investigate further into Brookfield's widow, as well. He assembled the team to kick around ideas, holding off returning phone calls from Trevor Coats, the San Joaquin County Sheriff, up for reelection next month. Coats had been leaving Ed voice mails and threatening all day to show up in person.

"Could be some kind of terrorist trying to ruin an American big business," offered Mendoza.

"Nah. Too tidy for that." Walt glared at her. He didn't think women should be cops. Period.

A phone call from Ron Tompkins, the General Manager, got Ed's attention. After Ed told him the coroner had removed Brookfield's remains, the manager became incensed that customers were still being kept out of the store. He demanded they finish up, so he could get a 24/7 crew in to clean up. He wanted to reopen in the morning. "This is killing our business. You have any idea how much we lose each day we're closed? Headquarters is flying out an attorney to handle our rights."

Ed realized that gossip and news coverage were already inflaming the public. Past, present, and future customers—wriggling with rumors—crowded three and four deep at the front store windows, trying to get a glimpse of the hubbub inside. They circled the parking lot, driving from one media van to another, trying to get interviewed or even be seen waving in a background shot.

"Sorry, Mr. Tompkins, we can't let anyone in yet. We're still working the scene. We've got most of the department on it." Ed didn't want to mention Sheriff Coats might call in the FBI, bring in the big boys to get this thing solved. It would make him feel powerless, again.

"If this draws those crazy anti-global demonstrators or union folks out of the woodwork, our attorneys are going to lay it on you." Tompkins hung up.

"Let's get back out to Morada." Ed punched Walt in the shoulder and yanked on his overcoat in case the autumn evening air turned nippy, thinking of the weather forecast for rain. "Check out Brookfield's peeper venue in the dark, see if there's any action. That widow of his shows too much sweetness and light, you ask me."

TEN

A Secret

HILLARY DROVE UP TO THE COLLEGE. Her stomach growled, but she had no appetite. *Maybe witnessing that horror will help me stick to a diet. Got to lose these pounds or I'll face the same heart attack trip Daddy did. Maybe younger.*

She was shocked to learn that the student staffers—focused on their own stories—hadn't heard about the PriceCuts killing. She needed to lecture on ways to keep in touch with the local goings on, not stay so isolated. But, she'd had enough and figured they weren't ready for the dismemberment story breaking into their weekly *Delta Breeze* plans, so she didn't let on. It was good to forget about it, even for a brief time, and return to the advance story of the Jacki Jones visit. The students were focused on the celebrity designer coming to town next week to open her line of home furnishings and her high tech marketing system.

Tiny Clearwater was smack in the middle of a customer base stretching from Sacramento to Stockton. The student art editor had created a clever graphic showing PriceCuts at the center of a shoppers' bulls-eye. A couple staff writers had worked for days to firm up their report on Jacki's business dealings. She'd gotten caught in a legal snafu and been escorted into a high-class federal prison a couple years ago but released on good behavior after a year served. The other student writers had collaborated on a series of sidebars detailing Jacki's business successes over the years and her advice to young people about taking on the world as entrepreneurs.

They had been working most of the day in the journalism classroom, converted into a sort of city room. Instead of scrawny tablet arm desks as in typical classrooms, they had office desks with drawers, topped with donated Dell computers, to simulate a real newsroom.

Hillary sat brooding at her faculty advisor desk as they finished up their stories and got them ready to copy and paste into the desktop publishing software the college print shop used.

Out of nowhere, the student copy editor asked Hillary about plagiarism, a simple technical question on quotation marks. She searched her tired brain to come up with the standard, English Department-approved message. The faculty this year were flying high on a witch-hunt over the issue. Damn them anyway. *Think they're so perfect. I'd love to see one of them under the pressure of a deadline in the real world.* Would it never fade? The fear of Charles noticing her success, if he did, and spreading around what she'd done charged her feet with a quicksilver itch to run south of the border, far away, anywhere that had no newspapers. As if there was such a place.

With the students' attention back to finishing up their own work, she googled her byline. Nothing shameful popped up. So far. After Charles caught her that last panicky time, she'd decided to leave New York, content with a master's degree in hand, and forget about going for a job on the east coast, much less staying on at Columbia for a Ph. D. She couldn't help it. The compulsion only hit once in a decade or so—didn't mean she was a thief, did it?

Hillary felt a mixture of relief and disappointment that the detective hadn't shown up yet for more questions. Had he been coming on to her? She needed the attention now more than ever. After the students put the paper to bed, she walked the dimly lit corridor with them, away from the *Delta Breeze* newsroom. She had parked in the faculty lot, so she veered off and hurried out to her car this October evening, grown muggy and threatening to rain. Looking across the lot in PriceCuts direction, she felt grateful for their halogen lamps, set up to make customers forget time, like a casino having no clocks and lit up at all hours. Halloween Sale posters dotted the superstore walls. She usually looked forward to Halloween, her favorite holiday when masks and cover-ups were the norm.

Last week, the students had run an article on how friendly PriceCuts was as a neighbor to the college, letting students park free in their lot at the crowded start to the fall semester. Hillary tried to keep an open mind, but she felt for the local shop owners getting squeezed out by the big-box retailer, even if PriceCuts had set themselves outside the town proper, in the rural area where land was cheaper. Customers didn't seem to mind driving out there, the prices were so good. Many of them were house poor from paying close to a half-million for a house in the new tracts that were springing up like mushrooms after rain, swelling the area's combined population over the fifty thousand mark.

There were few cars tonight in the PriceCuts lot, she noticed. The store must be still closed. She sat in the Golf's leather seat, exhausted, couldn't move a muscle. The memory of what Charles had done washed over her. His threats back in New York. She felt squished, like some kind of worm out on the sidewalk after a rainstorm. It was her good fortune he didn't carry through and report her. Columbia could have make a public example of her as part of their investigation of that assistant professor who was plagiarizing all over the place and smudging Columbia's reputation for spotless ethics.

She shook herself back to the present. Better call and let that detective know she wasn't waiting around at the college for him.

ELEVEN

A Chase

ED AND WALT DROVE PAST a couple of Morada estates, set back from the road and obscured by the leafy cover provided by ancient trees. Going by the Brookfield place, Ed slowed to a crawl, made a U-ey, and drove by it again.

"Doesn't look like any party tonight." Walt gestured toward the dark mansion.

Bright light shone from a single window in the upper right corner, the master bedroom Ed had observed on his earlier visit, a bull's-eye from the peeper's point of view.

Pulling over to the side of the road, they got out of the unmarked and walked alongside the fence, peering in the dark to check for shapes or movement, anything in the vicinity of the double mattresses.

"No one's there, unless they're lying down—or awful damn dusky," whispered Walt. "We walk in, the crunching leaves give us away."

Ed flicked the beam of his flashlight toward the mattress. A slim form jumped up and sprinted away, toward the open land of the drainage easement.

The detectives rushed after the figure, heedless of noise now that their prey was on the run. At the rear of the Brookfield place, he took a sharp right, avoided running into the storm drain field, and darted along the back side of homes and vacant lots, some fenced and some not. Impaired by years of fudging on their fitness, Ed with cigars and Walt with sweets, they lost sight of the fleeing form and ended up on one of the country lanes winding through the trees. Dotted with cottages and sprawling ranch-style homes, the eclectic neighborhood of Morada was settling down in the cool night—all except for the guy that got away.

"Damn. Time to tell the Widow Brookfield she's had company." Ed stared at Walt.

"Could be she already knows?"

"Wouldn't put it past her, could even be in cahoots with him, but still, we're obliged to notify." Ed dialed the cell number she'd given him. No answer. He left a message to phone ASAP. They made their way back to the car through vacant lots, along train tracks and easement land, starting to set to memory the layout of Morada.

Ed's cell rang. It was Hillary telling him she'd left college and gone home.

"We're out here in Morada now," he said, feeling drawn to her even though he knew better than to mix pleasure with business. "Mind if we come by? Got something you need to know."

"I'm pretty tired," she said, "but okay. Got my address?"

"Yup, took it down this morning. See you in a few."

Walt let loose his loud belly guffaws, sounding like a moose in heat bellowing in the woods. "You're looking for some oral gratification to replace those cigars you gave up, can't fool me."

Ed ignored the implication—Walt could be so crude. "You know what you need to give up, buddy, and get to the gym. It's a sin and a shame, the condition you're in."

TWELVE

A Warning

A TRIM VW GOLF and a classic white Mustang were parked in a clearing at the side of the structure. With no garage, Hillary's cottage looked like an old carriage house. Ed banged the brass doorknocker, pretty sure he had the right place. He glanced at his watch. He didn't mind how late the hour was getting. He knocked again.

"See any life over the top of the curtains?" he asked Walt, who shook his head and smoothed his hands down over his belly. Ed frowned and leaned forward for the thick brass ring, nearly falling off balance as the heavy oak door swung open.

She stood in the entry, clutching the doorknob, a smaller figure than he remembered. He realized she looked enough like him to be a cousin, for God's sake. He didn't want to make this any worse but had to warn her there could be a pervert in her neighborhood.

"Can we come in?"

She nodded and led them into an open room, gesturing over to a man who was tossing strands of pasta as if it were a salad. "Meet Roger, my buddy and boss. A man of many talents. He came to cook for me," she said. He nodded at the detectives as she went on talking. "We filed the PriceCuts story, and I got the kids' paper to bed. Wowza!" She raised her shoulders and let them drop, her arms dangling at her sides.

The air was heavy with garlic. "Do you like Italian?" She sat down at a thick wooden plank of a table.

Ed and Walt remained standing. "Sorry to interrupt your dinner," Ed said, "but we wanted to alert you. There could be a peeping Tom here in Morada. Might be set up outside the Brookfield place. Those cowards don't usually do anything but watch to get their jollies, but . . ." He felt a flush of embarrassment fall over his face. *Jeez.* "Still, it wouldn't hurt to keep your doors and windows locked, maybe cover them up if you can." He motioned toward the windows.

"Shades of Lady Godiva." Hillary gave a nervous giggle. "One of you guys could have been the peeper. With these café curtains, anyone can look in through the tops." Her gray eyes opened wide.

No dimples. Had I imagined them? "Well, of course," Ed gestured with open hands as if offering a gift of the air, "they rarely knock, and you're not out riding your horse, so not much danger, but . . ." *Can't believe what I'm saying.*

Frowning, she dragged her fingers through her thick red hair and looked over at Roger. "Do you think your landlady aunt might spring for some new window coverings? My karate won't do me any good if someone sneaks in while I'm asleep. Besides, I've never had to use my 'kee-yah!'" she yelled out the energy breath, "in real life!"

Roger set a creamy pasta speckled with green on the refectory table that separated the compact kitchen from the living room. "I'll ask her when she phones from her next port of call, but go ahead with it, sure."

He waved his hands over the food as if floating a whiff of temptation through the air toward the detectives. "Care to join us, officers?" He smiled, pulled out a chair, and stood like a genial host, waiting.

"Thanks, we're not supposed to eat on the job, but mind if we ask you a few questions?" Despite the presence of her editor, Ed was flooded with a powerful urge to stay and protect her until the peeper was captured and they found out if he was connected to the Brookfield murder. *Another killer on the loose—you've got to get the son of a bitch this time.*

Roger placed more pasta bowls on the table and sat down to serve his hot linguine with pesto.

"Now you've had more time, you recall any thing else you might have heard or even smelled while you waited for your interview with Brookfield this morning?" Ed asked, his stomach giving a noisy gurgle, stimulated by the aroma of the fragrant pasta.

"It feels like a hundred years ago." She swirled a few strands around on her fork.

"Hillary, have some of the white Zin. It's nice and light. You've had a brutal day. Officers, sit please." Roger was charming, reminding Ed of the way Brookfield himself had been described.

"So." Prolonging his stay, Ed sat and turned to the man she had described as her editor. *What was their relationship?* "Did you know Brookfield?"

"Sure. Knew him way back in his carefree time in San Francisco, before he put himself on the straight and narrow. And I interviewed him for an advance series when they were building PriceCuts last year. Covered the design work, what shoppers could expect."

"What kind of design work?"

"Well." Roger refilled his wine, swirling the light pink liquid around in the stemmed glass. "Poor Steven was more sociable than most PriceCuts execs, but oddly paranoid at the same time. He and Tompkins had that inner sanctum room built in, somehow managing to get headquarters to foot the bill for security features like those at the home office. You know, in case of trouble here. All those demonstrators. I couldn't put that in the article, of course, and the conference room sure didn't save Steven." He shook his head slowly.

Hillary choked on her wine and spit pale fluid out over her barely touched bowl of linguine. "You knew about that room I got lost in?" She grabbed her napkin and clamped it to her lips, then scraped back her chair and ran out of the room.

Ed wondered what was going on with her. *Can't follow her in the middle of questioning him.* He felt pulled in two directions.

Roger frowned in a sort of apology and picked up the wooden serving spoons to give the pasta another toss. "Sure you won't have some?"

"No, thanks." Shaking his head, Ed asked, "So did you ever go to any of those Brookfield parties?"

"Only showed up for business, background material. Never got involved, too close to home, you know." He swirled strings of pasta around his fork and wrapped his mouth around it with gusto.

"Anyone you see at the parties who seemed to have a thing out for Brookfield?"

"Well, his wife, of course. She had her eyes on him all the time, even when she had her lips locked on someone else. You know the kind—I want mine and yours too, that insatiable femme type. And . . ." He paused to take another bite.

Ed scrawled onto his notepad, noticing the tension of the day had ratcheted up to push him beyond hankering for a cigar. Wouldn't hurt to pick up some Jack Daniel's on the way home tonight, if he ever got home. "And?" he prompted Roger.

"And, there was that night last summer when Steven got too close to Dr. Zasimo's wife. You'd never know such a mild-mannered optometrist could get so enraged."

"How so?"

"After he saw them coming down the outside stairs together, the doc pulled Steven away from his wife and punched him in the chops so hard he fell into the swimming pool. Cooled off his business, if you know what I mean. I know Zasimo has been in this country for awhile and seems like a good guy, but . . ." Roger wiped his lips, licked them and wiped again.

Ed wrote fast, not certain what all his young rookie had learned from the interview with the doctor that afternoon. "Where's Zasimo from?"

"I think maybe Pakistan," Roger said. "Only talked to him a couple times."

"Were there others at the parties or at work who would have reason to harm Brookfield?"

"The meat market manager, Stoner I think his name is. Had an ugly look going every time we met in that conference room for interviews. Never saw Stoner at a party. Wasn't one of the guys."

"We may need to talk to you later. We can reach you at the *Acorn*?" Ed put his notepad and pen into his coat pocket.

"At my downtown office." Roger fished his card out of a shirt pocket, and handed it over. "We're putting ourselves on the map starting with the ice cream terrorists down the road, and now this right here in our little Clearwater."

Ed warmed with pleasure to see Hillary return to the table and sip at her wine. Her face looked pale. She didn't touch the food grown cold on her plate.

He stood and moved toward the door, with Walt following. Ed turned to look squarely at Hillary. "Be sure to lock the house. Wouldn't hurt to put something over the top half of the windows, too."

Roger looked at her, sitting with slumped shoulders at the table. "She's stronger than she looks. Trained in karate at Columbia. After 9/11 they made all students prepare for the worst." He showed the detectives to the door and gave a quick shake of his head. "But I'll hang out here tonight on the sofa." He smiled at her across the room, but she remained expressionless. "Don't worry. We'll call you, detective, if anything odd happens."

Ed wasn't sure that their arrangement wasn't odd, in and of itself. Roger seemed protective, but her body language told him nothing. Ed hadn't seen sight of her dimples here either, though the shock of witnessing discovery of those cut-up parts might be setting in hard tonight. A delayed reaction. Pretty normal. *Got to get that madman before he strikes again.*

THIRTEEN

A Meeting

HILLARY SLEPT PEACEFULLY knowing Roger was out on the sofa, just in case there might be some threat from a possible peeper in the neighborhood. The next morning, they drove their separate cars over to *The Acorn* office to get to work on the Brookfield obituary. Not only was Roger her editor and owner of the paper, the two of them had connected right from the start in their undergraduate days at Sacramento State University. Later, they both wrote for the local papers until she packed herself off to graduate school in New York. When she moved back home, master's degree in hand, Roger welcomed her with open arms at the small-town weekly he'd inherited from his grandfather.

This morning Roger started a pot of French Roast at the wooden counter running along the back wall of the office. Mildred, his late grandfather's girlfriend over the last decade of his life, came in around noon to help out as a volunteer. She said it helped her not feel so alone. The other staffers were stringers paid by the piece or just for the joy of getting to see their bylines.

Hillary loved the slow pace of the region, punctuated every so often by big stories she'd found when looking through the old *Clarion* files. Articles covering winemakers and their exploits over the years. No time for searching anymore. This crime focused all her attention on the killer and his victim.

She moved her chair over to sit beside Roger's antique roll-top desk, and the two of them settled in over fresh coffee to brainstorm ideas for the obituary.

"Got to pull in the sex party angle." She took a handful of peanut M and M's from the bowl on his desk and tossed a few into her mouth. "Chocolate and coffee, two food groups for the morning."

He licked his lips and laughed. "Can't include orgies in an obit. We aren't the *National Inquirer*, Dopey."

She wrinkled her nose at him. In college, they were in a group—seven student writers under the tutelage of a retiree from the *Christian Science Monitor* who insisted the sunny side of stories should balance the dark. Roger had anointed them with seven-dwarf names, and theirs had stuck over the years since graduation. She hated being called Dopey, but after what she'd come to recognize as her "P problem," she suspected she might deserve the moniker.

Roger loved writing obituaries—a type of feature writing feeding his penchant for dashing off short stories. They shored up his aim to stretch out into writing novels one day.

"What've you got so far?" She took another handful of M and M's.

"Looks like his HR job with PriceCuts was the highlight of his business career." Roger handed her a thin stack of printouts he'd gathered about Steven Brookfield. "He was in the tabloids a lot after his marriage to wannabe celeb Belinda. I knew him in his wild oats days in San Francisco's Castro. Bisexual. There's never a mention of any kids."

"Shooting blanks?" She leafed through Brookfield's slim biog file.

Roger shook his head. "Dunno."

"Well, Belinda's fertile years were behind her, for sure." Hillary flashed on her own situation—never married and childless at thirty-five. She pulled her hair back into a twist and stuck a fat black pencil through it to hold it in place. "What's the plan for the funeral?"

He raised his dark eyebrows. "Let's go talk to widow woman and find out. Bring your camera today, Dopey." He grinned as she stuffed it into her overflowing tote.

They left the one-story building on Main Street and got into his Mustang. As he revved up the engine, Hillary got her Powerbook out of her bag. Despite its weight, she'd decided to keep it handy. She read through the articles she'd downloaded earlier for more details about Brookfield as Roger drove the few miles south into Morada's orchard-turned-estates territory. The narrow road was spotted with media vans parked near the Brookfield place.

"Got to park down aways," she said, directing him to a spot not far from her cottage. Roger pulled over to the side of the narrow lane and fit into a space on the skimpy shoulder. As they walked back to the estate, Hillary offered more background information she'd dug up on the Internet. "He was her seventh spouse. She had this mansion built as a wedding gift for him a couple years ago but told everyone he'd done it for her. She took his name for the alliterative BB initials—Belinda Brookfield." They threaded their way among vehicles, peeking into RVs crammed with equipment and monitors.

TV cameras were hoisted above the fence line to get clear shots inside the grounds. Framed in one of the RV's monitors, Hillary could see Belinda holding court inside. "We're late. Come on, let's go talk to glamour puss herself."

They flashed their press passes at a security guard standing at the gate. The massive front doors were wide open, flanked by skimpily dressed maids greeting members of the press and showing them into the living room. A young Latina ushered them in, waited for a pause, and interrupted the widow's Q and A session. "Mr. Ingram, Ma'am, about *The Acorn* obituary."

In a honeyed tone, the widow called to the maid: "We're all friends around here. Call me Belinda. Or even nicer, call me 'Belly.'" She winked at the young woman. Shifting her attention to Roger, she smiled. "I love our local press!" She held out a hand, palm down, as if for a kiss.

Ignoring the offer, Roger whipped out his notebook. "Mrs. Brookfield—"

"Belly, please."

"Belinda. Have you got anything you want us to run besides the information published when Mr. Brookfield was added to top management with PriceCuts?"

"Oh, darling, it's so kind of the paper to run a story on him. Be sure to say Steven was . . ." The widow's lavender eyes, courtesy of tinted lenses, watered up. She patted under each eye with a silk hanky. "He was . . ." She sank onto a suede banquette. "He was so, so . . ."

Roger waited, left thumb clenched to secure his tape recorder on top of his notebook, right hand holding a pen poised over the page.

Hillary stood to the side and took photos of both the widow and the other media reps in the room, impatient as sharks when chum has been thrown into the water. The story of the news coverage would be as engaging as the killing itself, for their readers.

"Understanding. Yes. That word describes him." The pop culture wannabe dabbed at the corners of her eyes, then walked to a massive mirror hanging over a tall marble fireplace. After batting her lashes in the mirror, she threw her right arm up onto the mantle.

"Understanding." She lowered her head onto her forearm, causing several digital flashes to burst at once from cameras in the room.

Roger paused five or ten seconds. "Understanding?"

"Yes. Understanding." Belinda whirled to face him. "He was not from my world. But he learned what I needed and wanted."

No one breathed.

Roger voiced the question hanging in the room. "Which was?"

"Well, freedom, you know. Freedom and security. I wanted it all and he . . . he learned to give me what I needed. But look now, look at this ending." Her shapely frame shook with the motions of sobbing as if in a silent movie. Hillary wondered if she herself could pull off such an act if she ever needed to.

Belinda turned away for a moment before resuming her pose. "Don't forget to put that in the obituary—he was a perfect husband, the best." As if overcome with grief, the new widow reached out for a nearby domestic in a French maid's costume and let the young woman escort her out of the room, parting the gathered witnesses to her drama. The two mounted the wide staircase.

Before vanishing into her private quarters, Belinda leaned down from the second story landing. "Don't forget to say he leaves behind a much-beloved wife. For the first time, I'm a widow and not a divorcee, bless his heart." She smiled.

"Ma'am! Ma'am!" Roger yelled, jerking his head to motion for Hillary to come up the stairs alongside him.

Belinda frowned.

"What arrangements have been made? Is there going to be a funeral?" he asked.

"Certainly not. Steven would be turning over in his grave at the thought of a funeral."

He might turn over if he were all in one piece, Hillary thought, with a sickening lurch in her stomach.

The widow waved her arms, gesturing to the outdoors. "We will have a private cremation and then scatter the ashes here, have a farewell party for him, his final party. Steven loved these old trees, the smell of wet leaves in the fall."

She began to tear up. "He was not a man of organized religion but a man of love, not a mean or jealous bone in his splendid body." She disappeared down the hallway on the arm of her maid.

Hillary watched Roger scribble into his notebook: Party arrangements—TBA. "Let's get out of here," he said.

Hillary turned away and walked back into the living room. She began poking around behind the bar at the far end of the room, next to French doors that led to the patio and pool, sliding open a drawer at hip level, and spotting a baggie of marijuana.

"Can you believe it! They leave their drugs right out in the open," she said as Roger caught up with her. She was snapping photos when a young man dressed in all black, a vacant expression on his face, moved in to shut the half-open drawer and direct her out of the area.

"That's not what I would call out in the open." Roger nodded at the drawer as they left. "Come on. I want to wrap up this obit." They left the mansion, Hillary taking photos in all directions as they walked the driveway and the road leading back to Roger's car.

She felt wired. "Can't wait for the memorial party. Guess 'Belly' did love him in her weird way," she said. "She wouldn't have had him offed simply for the publicity—I don't think."

Roger glanced at her with narrowed eyes. "That grieving widow sure wants big time press coverage, but I agree, she's no killer."

* * *

Ultra jittery over her proximity to a peeping Tom, who might be one and the same as a murderer, Hillary talked Roger into staying over again that night since there wasn't time yet to go buy new window coverings. After they ate linguine leftovers and Roger's tossed green salad, she washed the few dishes by hand. Arms up to elbows in suds, she felt soothed by the hot soapy water.

Roger stood at the kitchen counter, sipping a local dessert wine and breaking off chunks of dark chocolate from a package open on the counter.

"Those cops seem like they're going in slow motion."

She frowned, "I need to get a move on, get tops for these café curtains in case the peeper runs amok in the forest."

"Don't get your panties in a wad, girl." He swirled the viscous wine in his glass.

"Help me put up pillowcases," she said, turning to face him. "Let's thumb tack them up in the bedroom, anyway."

Daylight savings was in effect for another week, so it wasn't getting dark early, but she felt a chill unrelated to the weather. She realized how sheltered a life she'd led, protected by her father and their suburban neighborhood. And then the cozy second-story Sacramento apartment with Tom—but getting engaged to that weirdo was sure a mistake—and the old-fashioned dorm at Colombia. "Please."

She took a couple muslin cases from the closet in the hallway, and waited for Roger to follow her. As they entered her bedroom, a feathery green limb hanging low from a redwood near the cottage sprang up toward the window. She jumped and dropped the pillowcases.

"Must have been a jackrabbit," Roger said, pulling shut the white cotton panels on the bottom half of the two windows. He picked up the pillowcases from the floor.

"There aren't any jackrabbits around here," she said.

He set to work thumb tacking the pillowcases over the windows, while Hillary stood frozen, picturing herself a human bull's-eye.

"All set now." He stood back to admire his work. "I'm here with you, anyway, so feeling better?"

She nodded, and they went back to the kitchen.

"Those cops, they've got to find who butchered Steven." He poured himself another glass of wine and sat at the table.

She finished the last of the dishes, turned off the water, wiped her hands, and joined him, ignoring the few crumbs left on the table. "What was Steven to you, anyway?" she asked, studying him as he sipped his wine. With surprise, she realized she knew almost nothing about his personal life over the last several years.

"I met him in San Francisco a couple years ago. He was cruising incognito, couldn't let the PriceCuts' honchos know this side of him. It was his flaxen hair and sapphire eyes that hooked me, plus his love of freedom and theatrics in the City."

Hillary sat and listened, fascinated to learn of his life in San Francisco, the edgy stories of the Castro District's wild side, not surprising for the City. *But here, things should be quiet and calm, boring even.*

Roger rubbed his face with both hands. "Yep. The City and the good old days." He walked to the sink, slugged down the last of his drink, and rinsed out his glass, swirling the water into a tiny whirlpool.

She stared at the blackness visible through the tops of the living room windows. No pillowcases to cover the café curtains there—not one star shone through this cloudy night. She felt like she was spiraling deeper into danger.

FOURTEEN

An Exchange

IN THE SHERIFF'S BRANCH OFFICE just outside Clearwater, Ed tipped his chair back at the desk he'd been assigned for this case, brooding over the rumors pouring in from all over San Joaquin County and beyond. They'd received so many tips, he worried they could never get through them all.

"Let's get someone from over at the college to send us a couple interns. You can supervise 'em." He meant it as a question but was so used to Walt agreeing with him, he put it as a statement.

Ed rummaged through the unfamiliar desk drawers. He found a thin local phone book, turned to the college numbers, punched in the AJ department's number and got a recorded invitation to leave a voice mail for the Administration of Justice secretary, which he did.

"Okay, so here we are, busting ass to keep a watch at PriceCuts, but no closer to solving the killing." Ed stared at his partner seated one desk over, and then rummaged around in the nearly empty desk drawers. He took one of his business cards and scraped out the detritus at the bottom of the shallow drawer just under the desk top, absently looking for signs of tobacco.

Walt pulled a tin of peppermints from his inside coat pocket, flipped open the lid to pop the last of the white disks into his mouth, and tossed the empty into the wastebasket. Talking through his chewing, he read aloud from the preliminary coroner's report on his desk, looking up to point at matching items printed in red marker on one of the few whiteboards on the wall.

"Killing and dismemberment of Steven Brookfield, Human Resource Manager. Time of death, between midnight and three a.m. Body discovered in his office. Place of death, most likely the same office. No forced entry. Cause of death, asphyxiation." Walt ran his finger down the report page.

Ed stared at the whiteboard, with narrowed eyes. "What's our angle?" He stood and stretched, arms reaching toward the ceiling, rotating his hands to loosen up his wrists. "We've been over and over this. Wish we could call in a Behavioral Analysis Team like on TV." He laughed a short bark. "Must be someone with access to the backstore, fact number one." He closed his eyes. "And that layout on Brookfield's desktop. Deliberate in the extreme. Six pieces laid out in two rows of three pieces each. Four arm parts and two twenty-dollar bills. What's it mean?"

Walt shook his head. "Very little blood."

"How could there be little blood?" Without leaving Walt time to get a word in, Ed ranted on, building up energy, feeling almost demented himself. "What's the motive? Some kind of personal vendetta? A revenge killing, something against PriceCuts? We've gone through that list of demonstrators during the months of construction. The lawyer who sued PriceCuts and lost. We've talked to most all the employees. So many staffers hated the big store coming in, but love the lower prices and shop there anyway." He dropped his forehead onto the gray desktop. "What are we missing?"

"Who, not what. Skill level." Walt chewed for a few seconds. "Not many people can carve up bodies that neatly. We've got to double check that list of employees, see if we've got them all—they take unpredictable days off, damn it. What about hunters? Taxidermists? The surgeons in town wouldn't be likely, unless they were affected somehow by the big store."

Ed sat straight up and punched Walt in the shoulder. "Which of them might have been? Maybe someone had ties to some of the small businesses? We need to follow up on that Dr. Zasimo. I learned that he was an ophthalmologist in Pakistan but couldn't get certified to practice in the U.S. He got the okay for optometry here though. So he's likely got surgical knowledge."

The landline rang. The AJ program department chair offered to send over some students to act as interns. Ed felt relieved. The kids could sort through tips pouring in from the media campaign asking for help solving the case.

"If we don't get any more killings, we have a chance to get a step ahead here." Walt opened the top drawer of the desk he'd been assigned and, scowling, pawed through rubber bands, thumb tacks, paper clips. He pulled out a rumpled roll of Life Savers from the back. His shoulders relaxed a bit as his pudgy fingers worked at the end to open the roll.

Watching him, Ed made up his mind to go buy some cigars, not to smoke but just to chew on. Couldn't hurt, might help.

It started to rain.

FIFTEEN

A Celebrity

HER NERVES JUMPING, Hillary listened to Jacki Jones' invitation to set up a meeting, away from the hubbub at the store. Hillary grinned as the celebrity told her to join her at the posh Woodbridge Country Club for brunch. "I'll get there early, so look for me in a booth," she said.

Hillary nodded into the phone. Who could miss the famous designer with her spiky black hair, her charismatic blend of savvy professional and baby-boomer trendsetter. "Okay, and I've got long red hair and will be wearing a sage green pants suit." No need to mention her generous size; she was also easy to spot.

* * *

The layout of the private club was a mystery to Hillary. But Jacki's beefy publicist, who looked like he doubled as a bodyguard, met her out in front and led the way to the celebrity, ensconced in an elevated booth.

"Sweetie face," Jacki called out. She remained seated but offered Hillary her hand as she neared what might as well be a throne, with wait staff hovering a discreet distance back. "Hillary, yes?"

Hillary nodded, shook Jacki's petite hand, and slid into the booth, impressed at the older woman's vigor. "The locals are excited about your coming to town, but I'm wondering what you think about the possibility that customers will stay away, worry about safety? After the problem Monday, you know?"

"I'm still on New York time, so I'll have lunch," Jacki replied, ordering the Greek Salad and a local Zinfandel from an attractive young waiter she called Matt. "Sweetie, people love a scandal. The only bad publicity is none at all. We've made a deal with *Architectural Digest*. We're going to offer a free copy and a twelve-month subscription to each customer who signs up for a JJL design plan." She pushed an unruly spike of hair off her forehead. "Then on our website, we'll show how to get that classy effect for a lot less money." She grinned.

"What do you mean by 'plan'"? Hillary opened her notebook and scribbled fast. She gave a sorry, not ready, shrug to the waiter, who nodded but stayed near.

"Research shows women who shop at PriceCuts crave an upper class lifestyle and feel entitled to it as well. But they need sensible prices." Jacki bit into a crostini, coated with Parmesan and parsley. "My new system will give them all that and more." She raised her glass of red wine toward Hillary. "I recommend the 7 Deadly Zins."

Hillary fingered the mint leaves in her glass of water while she studied the menu. After years of observing what alcohol did to her father, she made it a rule not to drink while on the job and ordered the club's special iced tea and a Salad Nicoise. The cute young waiter jotted it down and disappeared.

She turned to Jacki. "Not to be politically incorrect, but have you had a chance to notice how large some of the shoppers are? Can you rely on that flimsy furniture line PriceCuts has in stock to not drag down the quality of your JJL items?"

Jacki ignored the question and pressed on with her ideas while Hillary took notes. "With our new web-based software, it will be simple to create an individual design proposal for each customer, set up long-term buying plans, get them coming back for more—like a huge *House Beautiful* carrot they keep moving toward." She waved a bread stick in the air as if conducting an orchestra and flashed her spectacular smile at the waiter, who'd arrived with their orders. "Matt, darling boy! What fast service. You are a young superman, aren't you!"

Hillary's salad was set out in three sections on a rectangle of white china—a green bean, a potato, and a tuna stack. "I wonder if folks here are ready for such a high tech approach." She finished writing, set down her pencil and lifted a forkful of the tuna.

"Well, many people from the Bay Area have moved into the new developments all around here, since housing prices are so good; that will be a sophisticated segment of our customer base. Our next move will be to create a special issue of my JJL magazine, featuring layouts of local homes we've transformed. We'll be educating folks all over the valley—they'll love it." The glamorous designer, pushing birthday number seventy according to the tabloids, pulled a gold compact out of her purse and set it on the table.

"The model kitchen in PriceCuts is nearly done and we'll stock a higher end furniture line, too, for the generous-sized folks, as you asked about earlier." She smiled her brightest at Matt who refreshed her wine and refilled the club's apricot Rooibos tea for Hillary.

"Could I get more lemon, please?" Hillary asked. He nodded his sexy shaved head in her direction, and disappeared once more. She realized her heartbreak over Charles' betrayal had definitely faded away. At least in the romantic department. There was still a chance he could hurt her another way. She put a smile on her face to mask the grimace inside, picking up her notebook and nodding as Jacki continued outlining her vision.

"The demo rooms in PriceCuts are getting the finishing touches—would have been done today or tomorrow except for that unfortunate incident in the manager's office. Threw the whole place into a tizzy." Jacki opened the compact and checked her lipstick. "But, not to worry, it's already brought more Internet business after cable news picked up my reaction. The only thing worse than being misquoted is not being talked about at all," she said.

"Where did you hear that?" Hillary asked.

"Think I got it from your good old San Francisco Mayor Willie Brown. A star in the publicity heavens." Adroitly, she picked at a flake of parsley wedged between her teeth and flicked it away, snapping shut her compact. Hillary wondered if she had any green stuff in her own teeth and ran her tongue over them, hoping for the best. *Need to start carrying a mirror.*

"Speaking of free publicity, wouldn't hurt to plant a rubber finger from a costume shop in a package of PriceCuts chicken wings." Jacki laughed a horsey bray at the expression of shock Hillary couldn't conceal.

How had she found out about the fingers missing from Brookfield's hands, the kind of detail the detectives wanted to keep a lid on?

"Just kidding, Sweetie. The JJL Home Center should be in place soon. I'll phone you so you can be there when we drop the curtains and unveil it. Have any more questions?"

Hillary shook her head. Jacki had self-propelled her way through the interview, offering plenty of information. "I've got your number in case I need to follow up later."

Matt refilled Hillary's tea, dispensing in addition a hint of basil and lime cologne. She fantasized his forearms rippling under his white shirt.

"We'll each take a box, thank you." Jacki looked at the check and laughed. "Can you believe the price of food out here compared to New York? This place is such a rustic hideaway."

"It's not hidden any more after this killing—for better or for worse," Hillary said. "I'll get right on the JJL design center opening story. Let's pray it doesn't get topped by any more murders."

Hillary laughed, hoping she was indeed just joking.

SIXTEEN

A Married Couple

THE FOLLOWING DAY, Hillary finished the advance story on the JJL Home Center opening. Then she set out to cover the Harvest Fair, a faint echo of Lodi's September Grape Festival, one of many celebrations of agriculture in fertile San Joaquin County. Held in Clearwater College's parking lot, the Fair showcased walnuts, corn, and pumpkins among plentiful offerings from the rich farmlands. Hillary threaded her Golf through the parking lot. A couple media vans had set up earlier, the big-name news outlets on the hunt for developments in the PriceCuts killing.

She strolled past booths displaying goods from small ranches and orchards, all proud of their distinctive labels. The event resembled a farmers' market set up to showcase autumn harvest abundance. The aroma of roasting corn reminded Hillary she hadn't yet had more than coffee and a biscotti. At a Diamond Walnuts table, she bought a slice of walnut pie and savored it bite by bite as she wandered the fair.

Aisles set up in the parking lot filled with customers coming to check out October's prize-winning vineyards and taste the newly released vintages. In the relaxed atmosphere, she stopped to study a series of posters detailing the history of winemaking in the region. One showed wild grapes flourishing since the 1850s, growing in treetops alongside the Calaveras River. The area's Mediterranean climate of warm days and cool nights plus the deep loam soil, similar to France's Chateauneuf-du-Pape, created this perfect terroir for grapes like Zinfandel, Syrah, and other reds. The sophistication of marketing and public relations strategies by valley businesses impressed her.

Hillary's piece for the The *Acorn* began taking shape in her mind as she interviewed several members of a pioneer family who had transformed their roadside café and vegetable stand down on Highway 12 into Michael David Wines. As if showing off a new infant, they held up a bottle labeled Earthquake Cabernet Sauvignon and their old vines Lust Zinfandel. The savvy owners had remodeled their business—formerly known for its vast selection of dry beans—into a classy wine tasting room, complete with spitting buckets.

"How has PriceCuts affected your sales?" Hillary stood poised, pencil at the ready over her notebook.

Their proud smiles turned to frowns as they lamented that many wine converts were now driving north of Highway 12 to buy wines cheaper at the new superstore up in Clearwater.

Hillary sauntered along the rows of vendors, noticing a LOVE YOUR LOCALS booth, with a prominent anti-PriceCuts display. She approached its charts showing percentages of small business failures after big-box chains took root in a community. A short woman with white hair done in a long braid down her back stood outside the booth near a hand-drawn poster promoting a Mom and Pop March up at the state Capitol. The woman held a clipboard in her hands.

"How're you doing?" Hillary asked, noting a nametag introducing the woman as Sarah Stoney.

"Got a couple people signed up already. We're so close to Sacramento." Sarah displayed the list on her clipboard. "Better cover it, honey. Supposed to be bigger than Seattle back in 2001."

"You going?" Hillary asked her, thinking that she looked more like a sweet little old lady than an activist going to demonstrate on the Capitol steps. Hillary'd watched many a protest when tagging along with her father, back in the 80s.

"Sure." Sarah lowered her voice. "Too bad we didn't do more of this before they came and took over Clearwater."

"We? They?" Hillary asked.

"My husband, John." She nodded her head toward a tall man with a gray crew cut, standing nearby. "He can't protest in the open anymore."

"Why not?" Hillary hadn't pulled out her notebook, which sometimes stopped folks from talking, but her press pass dangled in clear view from its lanyard. She waited.

Sarah positioned her clipboard near the side of her face, providing a cover. "Don't quote me, but even though PriceCuts didn't make him sign an agreement, they've been clear—no negative comments or complaints are allowed. And God forbid anyone who seems to be trying to unionize. That's a sure way to get fired. Not that John ever believed in unions anyway."

Hillary nodded, and pulled out her notebook and pencil.

Sarah pursed her lips and looked down. "Don't use my name, but we were forced out of business a couple months after PriceCuts came to town. John feels humiliated to have to swallow his pride and go to work for them, but we never saved up enough to retire on, always plowed it back into Stoney's Market. It's a sin and a shame."

Hillary nodded, jotting down details of their business and thinking there was something appealing about this woman.

* * *

As she prepared to leave the Harvest Fair, Hillary went into a bathroom in one of the nearby college buildings. She was surprised to see the white-haired woman at the sink, smoothing her wiry hair with fingers wet from the running water. The water brought out black streaks still shot through her white hair and suited her dark skin tones, thought Hillary.

Suddenly, the older woman whispered to her. "Meet me for coffee tomorrow morning?"

"Pardon?" Hillary knew better than to turn down sotto voce invitations. Plus, she felt a strange connection to this woman. "Where?"

"How about Little Joe's."

"Off Main Street?"

"Yes. See you around ten?"

After Hillary nodded, the older woman patted her on the arm. "My own daughter lives so far away. Thank you, honey girl."

Hillary rushed into a stall and pushed the door shut, wondering what this woman's issues were. She suspected something was very wrong with this picture. But what?

Rub-a-dub-dub,
Three men in a tub
And who do you think they be?
The butcher, the baker,
The candlestick-maker;
And all of them went to sea!
—Anonymous Nursery Rhyme

SEVENTEEN

A Second Lesson

IT MADE MY VEINS RUN ICY. Sales had gone up since the Brookfield lesson, not down. When I pushed carts of meat out to refill the white porcelain cases, the aisles were clogged with customers, each one looking like a sheep. A simple-minded follower. Couldn't fail again. Had to get the message across. Be more in their faces. Have to get more media attention. Perfect timing with this Jacki Jones hoopla coming.

Got to interest John in taking a look at some mechanical problem, something I suspect's wrong with the bandsaw in the backstore.

I tossed from one side to another, rumpling Mother's chenille bedspread, its nubs worn thin. She always forced me to nap before any big event, here on her soft bed, but the cancer had cut down her life. I tried to imagine her slim hand soothing my jumpy nerves as I figured how to right the wrongs visited on our town. Mother had a kind heart, but she would understand this was justified. Necessary.

Resentment and rage swelled every cell of my body. I was doing this for the little guys, the helpless ones, mortified by big companies who sent lackeys with layoff notices blaring, "You don't count anymore. We have to downsize, nothing personal. Your work has always been good." It was not that different from what John had said to me that awful day in the backstore of Stoney's Market. The heartless coward.

Pulse pounding, I jumped up, straightened out the worn bedspread, and stomped down the hall, papered with narrow green and white vertical stripes. I filled the freestanding sink with cold water and submerged my face, holding my breath until I thought my lungs would explode. This is what it would feel like tonight for that traitor Stoney. Thank God the honchos only cared about their own executive offices, and were too cheap to put the new security system into the regular backstore where us peons slaved away.

I stood and swiped the dripping water back over my hair, gazing at the medicine chest mirror, and visualized the past, picturing shoppers lined up at my white porcelain meat case back in Stoney's Market. Back in the good old days.

"How do you like those babies?" I'd ask, slipping my hand under a couple fresh-cut pork chops nestled on the shiny side of the butcher paper. As soon as the customer's eyes lit up, I'd whisk the glistening cuts over to my chopping block. Folding up one corner of the butcher paper at a diagonal, then crossing the sides over nice and tight, I'd roll up the package and tuck the last corner under moistened white paper tape. As the last step in the dance, I inscribed the price onto the matte finish of the paper, pushing hard with a black grease pencil. After smiley faces became popular, I would scrawl *mel* in lower case cursive under the price, punch in two dots and add a curved swoop with the grease pencil to create a tiny smiley face under wavy hair.

It was the best of times—our little shops. The butcher, the baker, the candlestick maker. *Life can be like that again.*

Looking down at the chipped spot on the porcelain, I dried the sink with one of Mother's eyelet-edged hand towels, folded it in thirds lengthwise and hung it over the brass ring. Humming "Rub-a-dub-dub" under my breath, I zipped down two flights of stairs to Father's basement workbench.

The Nike bag bulged with its black nylon authority, loaded with tools to get the job done. Phase two, Mr. John Stoney by name, Meat Department Manager by title. Well, technically a trainee, but soon he would be one of the honchos himself. *If I didn't put a stop to it.* I would lay him out as object lesson number two, piece by piece. All except his heart. First Brookfield's head, now Stoney's heart. Had to demonstrate what was needed but absent from these men who should have been doing battle with the monster retailer. Should take his guts instead of his heart, but that was too messy, repulse the public instead of offering the moral of the story. Presenting him heartless would be a clearer message than gutless. That I Ching trigram for Brookfield was too subtle for them even though the meaning exploded in my mind when I discovered it. Kun. Six pieces laid out in three rows of two parts each: once a choice is made, it is done and you are transported to a higher level of responsibility. Perfect. Except none of them got it. This time, the meaning of a missing heart would be unmistakable.

I unzipped the bag to take a final inventory. Laying out each tool one by one on the rough workbench, I hefted it and moved it through its motions, humming. These would cut down Stoney and the giant store. Both. I looked over to the corner to see if Mother was rocking in the stick chair. Nothing.

Crap. I forgot to pick up her wig from behind the Epsom salts. Got to do that soon as I get the chance, at break time. Being careful with my schedule had let me slip through the cracks of the detective interviews. So far.

EIGHTEEN

A Suspicion

HILLARY ARRIVED at Little Joe's and ordered a chai latte as a change from her usual French Roast. The only customer in the small coffee shop, she took her hot drink and sat down in a booth. She kept her notebook in her tote, considering this date with the woman from the Harvest Fair as an informal personal chat. So far.

A few minutes later, Sarah walked in, brushing rain drops off her white hair. She ordered a plain black coffee, and scooted into the booth, talking as she moved across the leatherette seat. "Hi, Honey. I could see you caught on about John, the way he was acting yesterday."

"No. I just saw him standing at the booth, looking at the people pass by," Hillary said.

"I'm worried about him, real bad."

"Why?" Hillary spooned off foam from the latte and savored its fluffy texture.

"He's not the same man since he had to close his little market, you know." Sarah unbuttoned her yellow plastic poncho and patted at it with a paper napkin to soak up the rain.

Joe brought over Sarah's coffee and set down a dish of bite-sized chocolate chip cookies in front of her. She picked up two and popped them into her mouth.

"But he has a job at PriceCuts now, right?" Hillary blew on her steaming drink.

"Well, yes." Sarah paused a moment to chew and swallow before she rushed on with her story. "And I try to convince him he's lucky to have a job. But he hates that place so bad. He's had dreams of fighting them down in the dirt—the owners out in Iowa, two brothers, you know. Dreams they are fighting in a huge cornfield. Every night." She hadn't touched her coffee. "He yells and punches the air in his sleep, so I'm scared he'll hit me. It makes me go sleep in our daughter's old room."

"Um," Hillary said, picking up one of the tiny cookies. "He wakes up angry?"

"Not at me, but he tells the fighting details at breakfast, getting so upset he can't finish his bacon and eggs. Says he knows he's going to lose in the cornfield, two against one and all. It's been months now and he sits and broods, saying he's nothing but a failure." She sighed and looked around the coffee shop. "I feel like it's my fault for not trying harder to save Stoney's Market."

"What did you do there?" Hillary felt around for her notebook and set it out on the table.

"I made up our weekly ads for years, stuffed into the *Clarion News*, back before you came, before the paper changed names. That's all the advertising we needed for decades. Didn't even need that back when John's parents were running the market. Everyone for miles around just shopped with us." Sarah sighed. "He's not the same man anymore."

"How did you and John meet?" Hillary doodled circles inside squares on her notebook, not sure if this was story material or not.

"John was deer hunting up near Shingle Springs and came into the Rancheria store looking for a skinning knife. His had broken. I happened to be in the store shopping for I forget what. He told me about his market down in Clearwater. How it sold the best meat on the west coast—kind of flirting with me, you know? A few weeks later I felt restless to leave the Rancheria so I got a ride down to buy meat. John was awful cute." She blushed. "He was bagging groceries and he carried out my stuff to the truck."

"What was he like in those days?" Hillary felt concern for this woman and it dawned on her that she must be about the same age as her own mother. Ever since her father died, questions about her mother had been creeping into Hillary's consciousness. She pushed those thoughts away, as usual. Was Sarah in danger?

"He was slow, steady, kind. Wanted his family's market to be an easy stop, handy for most things. Folks didn't need so much back then, not so many brands of everything, so many different products like now, you know."

"Did he have a temper?" Hillary smiled at Little Joe who'd come by to check on their drinks and nod at the full cups. He walked to the rain-glazed windows and stared out at the empty street, hands folded behind his back.

"A temper?" Sarah frowned. "Not to speak of, except when prices would go up. Later when superstores started building all over America, he did get upset. They built those huge stores out in the boonies and people would drive far to get those cheap prices. John couldn't understand it—why spend money on all that gas just to save a few pennies on cereal?"

Hillary sat doodling on her notebook, nodding at the tumbling flow of the old woman's worries, wondering what her own mother's voice sounded like nowadays.

"He never thought PriceCuts would come here, to our little town." Sarah squeezed her eyes shut for a couple seconds before she went on. "But after they did, our customers just quit coming. Each week we sold less, and even the meat counter's business fell off. John had to tell our checkers and baggers we were being forced to close." Sarah picked up her cold coffee and drained half the cup. Little Joe walked by and topped it off for her, keeping a respectful silence.

"Worst day of his life, the day he told Melvin—he ran our meat market for us. Their fathers started Stoney's after the Second World War. Come home neither of 'em wounded too bad and willing to work hard. Never had enough money to buy their own building. Kept prices low as they could." Sarah lowered her face to blow on her coffee, her silence measured by a pulse in her temple.

Hillary waited a few moments before she prompted her to continue her story. "So when was John born then, after the war?"

"In 1947, yep, so he's going to turn 60 in a couple years but now he's acting like he's 80, at home in bed when he's dreaming and not dreaming, if you know what I mean." She sighed and rubbed her fingertips around in small circles on her cheeks. "It's killing him. He thought he *was* the store. Since it's gone, he's lost."

Hillary frowned and sipped at her latte, grown cool. "How does he feel about the killing at PriceCuts?"

"That's the creepy thing. You'd think he would be happy, but no." Sarah sighed.

"Why would he be happy?"

"Well, to have doom come to the Goliath store, make him feel he wasn't alone in his misery. It made me feel like somebody wants justice, anyway."

"But John's not happy over it?"

"Feels the whole world's falling to hell, with the globals and the terrorists and all. He's ready to cash in his chips, is what he tells me. I'm worried he might do something dangerous."

"To himself?"

"Don't know, just have this twisting in my gut telling me bad times are coming."

"Could you stop him?"

"He doesn't pay attention to me anymore. It's like he blames me—it's taken the juice from his soul. He lived for that market, got up at four every morning to be there for deliveries, closed down at nine and came home with a heart full of energy. Would grab me and put on a record, dance around the house before sitting down to supper. He was a joy to be around, so funny. A people person all the way." Tears were sliding down her cheeks and she wasn't wiping them off.

Hillary felt sad for this loyal woman standing by her man all these years. Not like her own flighty mother running off from her father and her ten-year-old self. "Maybe we should run another story on PriceCuts' impact on small business?" Could that do any good, Hillary wondered.

"That's nice of you, honey, and what I thought I wanted." Sarah stirred the last three tiny cookies around on the dish. "But it might make him feel worse, now it's hopeless. That's what he is, hopeless, nothing to live for, just learning to run that big operation where everything shows up in case lots, gets moved around on the shelves so folks have to pass all kinds of impulse buys to find what they came in for. Huge packages making customers greedy to save a few cents." She pulled Kleenex out of the pocket of her poncho and blew her nose.

They were still the only customers. Hillary walked over to Joe's counter and asked for a refill. Colorful tissue-paper placemats strung together were swagged along Little Joe's walls. Tiny skulls and Dia De Los Muertos wording had been cut into the thin paper. Day of the Dead was coming soon. She sat back down across from Sarah, who was sipping at her coffee. Hillary waited for Sarah to carry on.

"He tries to put on a good front, but closing Stoney's took the starch out of his shirt. He's empty inside." Sarah frowned. "Maybe it would be good to write about the superstore killing the mom-and-pops, yes. How could things get worse? Honey, can you do that?"

Hillary swallowed and licked her lips, nodding. "I'll see what I can do."

Sarah gazed at the brown dregs in her cup. "Never thought it would turn out like this. Supposed to be golden years but it's nothing but pot metal, the way it is now."

Hillary wondered about her mother and how golden or tarnished her years might be. Was she still out on some island in the Pacific? Was she still alive? Hillary shook her head with a snap, well practiced at dodging away from consideration of those questions.

Instead, Hillary feared for this woman she had just met and wondered if she would be able to help her.

NINETEEN

A Warning

HILLARY DREAMED she was carrying gravel from her driveway, carrying it in a moccasin, selling it door-to-door. On a dark front porch, a black-haired stranger glared out from inside a narrow window. The window was smashed into dagger-like slivers barely clinging together. The stranger nodded at her. He parted his lips to display stained teeth and bent towards the window glass that multiplied his image into duplicates as if seen through a clear kaleidoscope. She felt drawn to push through that glass but instead stood on the porch, paralyzed.

She woke up confused and alarmed, trying to get back to reality. Then it hit her. Today was the Grand Opening of Jacki Jones' Home Design Center, and she was to cover the crazy hoopla PriceCuts had arranged.

Nerve cells fired through her brain. She jumped out of bed, knocking the digital alarm to the floor. Six o'clock. Two hours before the event started. She gathered her courage and drew back the muslin pillowcase covering the top of her window. The dark gray dawn looked thick with mist.

Yanking on her sweats and slipping into her old Pumas, she took a wake-up run through Morada. Keeping to the middle of the road, pepper spray in one hand, flashlight in the other, she kept a lookout for the peeper behind every tree. Her heart raced. She didn't need to slow down to a walk today.

Home safe, she reached into the bowl of dried orange peels and whole cloves she kept on the entry table. She stirred the potpourri, inhaling the spicy scent that meant fall. It was normally her favorite season. After turning on the coffee maker, she showered and put on a denim skirt, topped with a purple cotton knit sweater. Her black Doc Martens would be comfortable for this long day standing at the superstore. She sat for ten minutes in front of the unlit stone fireplace, savoring her hot black French Roast and sour dough toast.

At seven thirty, she drove out to PriceCuts, the rest of the coffee in her travel mug, but taking no biscotti today. Since last week, her stomach felt better when she left it on the empty side.

PriceCuts operated as a 24/7 machine, workers stocking merchandise onto the shelves from midnight to the eight o'clock opening and others selling it off the shelves and out the door from eight to midnight—all working hard and for the most part at a squeak above minimum wage. Employees were expected to put in overtime for no pay. It was hard to know what to make of the situation—she tried to stay objective, like a fair-minded reporter should, despite her sympathy for the workers.

A Jacki Jones JJL trailer was backed up to the loading dock platform alongside three or four other semis. A picture of aphids fastened to rose stems flashed through her mind, one of the many acrylics her mother had painted, all destroyed by her father over the years.

She shook her head and surveyed the competition. Several media vans were parked in the lot already but Hillary couldn't tell if any of the newsies had gone into the store yet. Roger was nowhere in sight although he'd said he'd be there before eight, take pictures of the doings. She knew he'd show up soon. She approached the back door guard station she'd passed through a week ago.

An image of the guy ahead of her in line last Monday flashed through her mind. She'd love to find him, just to know it wasn't a dream, find him and look at his shoes. Did he work here? Had the detectives talked to him? All she had to go by was the back of his head, the ashy dirt on his shoes and a glimpse of his profile. He seemed short, maybe an inch or two taller than her own five foot, eight inches. Short and wearing khaki pants with a long-sleeved pinkish shirt—kind of strange, a long-sleeved shirt in last week's Indian summer weather. It was hard to tell how old he was. He had nondescript dark hair, cut short. A dark brown leather belt. She tried to bring his image into sharper focus—did he have a mustache?

The guard at the back door was a different guy from last Monday. Some woman assisted him and they worked as a team, double checking IDs before letting anyone in. Hillary studied the half dozen folks in line but didn't recognize anyone.

Her turn came and she explained her situation. The guard wouldn't go for her press pass alone. He phoned Jacki inside the store and then Clarice—promoted from a glorified hallway monitor to an HR assistant in the shake up after Brookfield's death—to clear Hillary for opening day.

She rushed down the hall and out front into the vast retail spaces. Jacki was already there. "Hey, sugar!" she squealed, throwing her arms open as she spotted Hillary jogging toward her.

Jacki wore a silver stretch bodysuit, toned down by a floor length, quilted vest of velvet and silk squares in camels and grays. Very New York. Hillary grinned, feeling herself one of the designer's in-crowd.

"Time to show you the final preps before we open. Where's your photog?" Hillary said Roger would be there soon. None of the other reporters had been let in yet.

Jacki pointed to a nearby partitioned-off section of the store. "I'm going to open the wraps on the demo kitchen in a minute, do a preview for you." Canvas sheeting was positioned to keep the surprise element during construction, in the midst of store operations that had returned to normal.

After Brookfield's murder, lookie-loo curiosity and next-to-nothing prices brought customers back in bigger numbers than before. Hillary noticed many already lined up outside, for early bird give-aways on this special event extravaganza. There was to be a drawing for a whole houseful of PriceCuts JJL furniture.

Jacki hugged Hillary, kissing in the direction of both cheeks. "Watch me turn on the EasyCAD computers so people can transform their dreams into reality." She cha-cha'd over to three computer stations set up for customers. Anyone could create a computer-aided design floor plan by doodling onto the computer screen, turned Etch-a-Sketch for grown-ups and combined with the notion of a bridal registry. She switched on the control system and brought up the JJL basic house floor plan—cursors in the shape of pencils blinked in unison, ready for action. Hillary took notes and prepared herself for Jacki's preview opening.

Like a ringmaster in a circus with an audience of one, Jacki bowed in Hillary's direction and turned to gesture toward the canvas cloths hiding the demo kitchen like a theater curtain hides the stage. The drama queen designer pranced over and stretched up to take hold of the pull cord.

"Ta dah!" She drew the cord down in a smooth motion causing the fabric to swing sideways.

Hillary looked on, pencil poised over her notebook. As the sparkling new kitchen came into sight, Jacki let out a shriek of terror.

Hillary's jaw dropped open and her pencil fell to the floor.

"NO NO NO NO NO NO," Jacki screamed in an endless loop, while Hillary stood frozen in place.

She had only seen him once before but there was no doubt. It was Sarah's husband, John. Eyes open, his head faced straight out from its position on a black granite countertop, looking like a cookie jar in a horror movie. His naked torso sat upright in the adjacent stainless steel sink compartment, a wound gaping in the center of his chest. His arms, bent at the elbows, took up most of the space in the other sink. His legs stood on the honey-colored ceramic tile floor, parallel to each other and extending nearly up to the sink.

Hillary dashed into the backstore, frantic to find help. Clarice wasn't at her desk halfway down the hall. Hillary arrived breathless at the guard station, glad for the double staffing since the murder last week.

"There's a man." She pointed back toward the retail floor. "Get help," she gasped. "In parts. Kitchen sink. Call police."

The guard punched in 911 and then called for PriceCuts security backup. The woman on duty ran with Hillary out to the front of the store where Jacki seemed planted, motionless, her "No no no" quieted to a whispered mantra, a thin stream of drool running down the side of her chin. Hillary stood near, wondering if she should shake her. She reached out to touch the designer's thin shoulder, hunched inside her glamorous outfit.

Suddenly, Jacki regained her volume. "It's ruined our opening!" She ran to the phone at her demo kitchen desk. "I've got to get a cleanup crew in here." She began punching in numbers.

Hillary tried to look anywhere except near the sink. *Not again. Holy Mary, not again.* She should be writing down details but couldn't force herself pick up her notebook and pencil from the floor. Shoppers lined up at the front doors were frowning, looking at their watches, and peering in the windows, not realizing how lucky they were not to get in at opening time for line of sight to the demo kitchen countertop.

* * *

A few minutes later, sheriff's deputies swarmed the massive building and parking lot, armed with rolls of yellow tape, sending away shoppers lined up at the front doors and marking off the crime scene. Clarice rushed out, explaining she'd been in the conference room bathroom, and confirmed that the dead man was John Stoney, meat market manager trainee, who Hillary knew as Sarah's husband. What would this do to the fragile woman who'd poured out her worries in Little Joe's last week? Hillary felt bile rising in her throat, and gratitude that she'd skipped the biscotti this morning.

Ed and Walt showed up moments later, grim faced. "You seem to be a common denominator at these scenes, young lady." Ed folded in his lips and studied Hillary. "Maybe you're not so good for business?" His grimace telegraphed that he could be trying to lighten the shock, but his words stung. To cover her distress, she looked down to search for her notebook and pencil, annoyed at the attention she was getting from Jacki, as well.

"Oh, my God! You witnessed both these displays." Jacki's voice returned to a whisper. She doubled her quilted vest over the front of her scrawny chest, turned away from Hillary and announced to Ed, "JJL is sending people to clean up."

"Can't let them in until we process. You and this young lady come along with us." Ed led the two women through the store aisles back to the small accounting office.

Relieved there was no pink donut box this morning, Hillary tucked loose strands of hair behind her ears and tried to comprehend Ed's questions. "There was no blood on the canvas. Anywhere. Any idea how can that be?" He queried her about the killing as if she might know.

The cramped room filled with cops and brusque voices. Ed and his notepad seemed far away. He focused on the details of today's discovery, but when Hillary began to pick at the seams of her denim skirt, he said he would finish up with her later. She felt pure gratitude, protected like a little girl, when she would sit in a corner of one of the Assembly Hearing rooms at the Capitol, observing her father taking notes, his hand filling page after page in minutes. It seemed a wonder to her back then. *Notes,* she thought, *I've got to get going on this story.*

She left the accounting office and ran back toward the parking lot, swimming against the media tide and barely avoiding a Fox News Land Cruiser headed straight for her. Media vehicles jockeyed for parking spots, not even braking before releasing reporters and photographers. They converged at the latest murder site like sharks when bloody chum is tossed into the ocean.

Only there was no blood here—again, Hillary thought, worried the story was ballooning too big. Jacki Jones' coming to this little town had been of note, but combine that with two macabre killings during sweeps month—when TV ratings were measured—and the story exploded into a major one.

She bumped into Roger, who'd been running uncharacteristically late and was now struggling amidst the others to get in.

"You missed the chance to get first-off pictures of the kitchen," Hillary said. "But we can't run them anyway, they are so . . ." She rolled her eyes.

Roger nodded. "I'll stay and get what I can. You run to the office and fling up a thousand words to convey the picture." He ran with her to her car and slapped the side of the navy blue Golf, as if it were a horse he was pumping up to win a race.

She jumped in and started her engine, her gut clenching under the pressure of this deadline to scoop the story. Another exclusive on her hands. Charles would surely see this one. *Damn.*

PART II

June Gillam

TWENTY

The Pressure of a Deadline

ALL CHARGED UP but sagging inside at the same time, Hillary drove back to the office to tackle writing up kill number two. This latest story would get picked up all over the news, her Hillary Broome byline with it. Another exclusive. Maybe she should have changed her name. *Holy Mary, don't let Charles and his gang notice it's me,* she thought. *I can picture his glee at running the story of my lapse in a sidebar to this murder news. Wipe out my reputation in a flash.*

Roger had stayed at PriceCuts to get reaction and photos, so she couldn't bounce ideas off him. Sick and nervous, she felt tempted to google around to see how stories like this had been handled by others, but forced herself to stick to her own five Ws: Who. What. Where. When. Why. Never mind the How for this go round. She stared at the screen, paralyzed, as if waiting for today's stunning visuals to replay in her mind's eye. Instead, she got the other rerun, the horror show she wanted to keep shut up in her psychic basement.

* * *

Cold blood threaded through her veins that last day at Columbia. Hunched over a keyboard, she scrolled through the words on the screen. For this final part of her master's culminating project, she'd been assigned to write a story on the families of terrorists.

She'd done her interviews. The ones with the mothers took all she had to get through. What would her own long-gone mother think of things she'd done wrong? Most Muslim parents stayed pretty neutral about the bombings. But two women insisted they would be proud to have their sons die as martyrs. Or even their daughters. Proud. Not that different from what a couple fathers had said. Hillary typed up their reactions to a recent terrorist incident, another one thwarted.

Her final piece explored the views of Muslim families but needed a finish, something to stick in the reader's mind, a nugget that made clear this was not merely competent but a zinger of a story. Something to light up her advisor's eyes and prove that damn Charles wrong.

He'd been her champion among the east coast press contacts before rumors that the *L.A. Chronicle* was going to retire senior writers like her father. Then Charles dumped her overnight for a sexy applicant to next years' incoming class.

Hillary's terrorist story for the Columbia News Service was due in ten minutes but no kicker came to mind. If she couldn't do a great job on this piece, she was out of the running to get into Columbia's doctoral program in journalism. She walked to the whiteboard in the empty classroom and uncapped a bright red dry erase marker.

and then, and then, and then . . . she scrawled onto the board in loopy handwriting, trying to get a capper for her story.

The door to Charles' office slammed open, hitting the classroom wall. Police sirens wailed from outside his window, open despite the choking fumes of New York City traffic. He stood glaring at

Hillary's red writing on the white wall. "Five minutes, drop dead time. I've got ten bucks says you can't finish up, Hilly." He'd taken to calling her "Hilly" after dumping her for that hot young thing.

He tossed out a thin-lipped smile and disappeared back into the editor's office, returning to his buddies, all Harvard graduates like him. They were soaked in their snobbish, ivory tower ways. *Maybe I don't belong here at Columbia after all,* she thought.

The stench of her nervous sweat underscored how much this feature article for the Columbia News Service meant. She stared through the glass window to the student newspaper office. Charles and the other editors he palled around with were goofing off, done with their own assigned final stories.

Shoving her father's ethics into the cellar of her mind, she sat down and googled "Islamic terrorist threats," her fingers icy cold as they tapped out the keywords. The hits included one from an obscure paper out in Lodi, California. It was a case of a father and son, the father an ice cream truck vendor whose son had spent six months at an Afghan Islamic Religious School. A claim from an imam about the case resounded as a finish for her piece: "Fathers and mothers glow when sons sacrifice for Allah."

Lips dry, she moused to Select, hit Copy, and Pasted it into her story as if it were her own thought. She knew she would be taking a chance. Scraping her fingernails at the edge of her hairline, she sat back as her ring tone announced a call. The number showed it was from her father's Sacramento

Bureau office. She let it go to message, knowing he would be able to spot the guilt in her voice.

Charles opened the door again. "One minute, Hilly," he hissed. "One minute to save your place in the big time."

She raised her eyebrows high, and hit Send. "It's on your desk, Charles." The veins in her arms felt icy, as if she'd been transfused with mercury, dragging her temperature to freezing. *Dad can never find out,* she thought. She didn't realize the call she'd sent to message would be the last time ever she'd hear his voice.

* * *

Hillary shook herself out of that New York nightmare from the past, and plowed into PriceCuts kill number two story, one word at a time. *No need for brilliance,* she thought, *just get the damn thing done. Use that Butt Glue you hand out first week to your students—stick to your chair and write.* She wanted to run away, take off and drive straight south to Mexico. Instead, she finished the Stoney dismemberment story and fled home in her Golf to crash.

* * *

A knocking kept on and on and became a merciless pounding. In a stupor, she dragged herself off the couch to look through the peephole. Ed. She opened the heavy front door, wishing she were opening to a replay of today with a different ending down at PriceCuts.

"How you holding up?" Ed frowned and wiped his forehead with a tan plaid handkerchief then stuffed it into his breast pocket. "You've gone through a lot."

She stared at him. He's right. Both times I was hit right between the eyeballs with the mutilations.

He reached out. She leaned into his arms and let go, sobbing, without awareness.

They stood that way for ten or fifteen long seconds.

What a great dad he must be, she thought. *I don't even know if he has kids.* She pulled back and grabbed the corner of the handkerchief dangling from his pocket. Blowing her nose, she felt small and wounded.

"Sorry about that," she said, moving into the cottage and waving him inside. "What kind of fiend do we have hanging around here in our local superstore?"

He nodded but said nothing.

"I thought the killer could even be Stoney, and here he's today's victim. Any leads on the peeper?" she asked.

Ed sat at the table, and let his chin drop onto his clasped hands, shaking his head, looking nothing like a burly detective on a television show.

Wagging her head mirror fashion, Hillary allowed every cell in her body to sag and register the shock at a deeper level. Two killings—now they were past the hot story stage and into real danger to the community. *Who could be next?* Her stomach burned with fear and an odd hunger all at once.

She excused herself to pad the short distance to the bathroom, searched around for the bright pink Pepto Bismol bottle, shook it up like crazy, and took a big gulp. After splashing her face with cold water, she returned to find Ed still sitting in the same slumped position.

She rummaged around in the cupboard, searching for canned corned beef hash, wondering how in the hell she could be hungry, wishing she had the ingredients to make some soothing potato soup. "Lunch? What time is it?"

He had taken his spiral notepad out and opened it on the table. "We're talking to taxidermists and gun store owners that sell skinning and field dressing equipment. Lots of hunting in the foothills not that far from here." He stretched both arms high, then let them bend at the elbows, folding his hands behind his head.

"What about that eye doctor, Zasibo?" She was starting to suspect there might be a tie to the Lodi terrorists, although those folks were in jail since last summer. It would be such a weird connection to her shame at Columbia.

"Name's Zasimo. We've pretty much cleared him. I want to find that peeper guy."

She opened both ends of a can of Dinty Moore Hash, pushed on one of the metal ends, and shoved the tube-shaped hash out of the can—careful not to slash her fingers. She sliced the cylinder of compressed meat and potatoes into thick rounds. A far cry from the peppery corned beef hash at the Stage Restaurant in New York where Charles used to take her when he was still laying on the charm.

The mindless rhythms of cooking, from cupboard to counter to stove, were soothing. Nearly as soothing as a Jack Daniel's on the rocks. Might pour herself one. She looked over at Ed. "Can I get you a drink?"

"Not on work time." He closed his notepad. "Got to call Matt. Get him over here. Show him that pervert's mattress along the fence at the Brookfield place. Part of his training."

"Matt?" The rounds of diced meat and potatoes sizzled in the skillet as she flipped each one over.

"Out of the AJ program over at the college. Took him under my wing after he did a ride-along last week and already he's an intern. Bright kid."

Hillary placed a white plate dotted with circles of crispy hash in front of the detective. "Hope you don't take ketchup?"

"I shouldn't," Ed said as he picked up a fork and dug in. "Just take it straight, nothing on it. Maybe some eggs in the morning. Sunny side up."

"Ummm." Frying up the hash had spent all her remaining energy—she didn't feel like talking. She sat down with her plate and forked in mouthfuls of the ruddy hash, groaning with pleasure over the chewy feel of it. *I could never become a vegetarian,* she thought.

After he finished, Ed sat silent at the table, looking at her as she ate. She absorbed his warm gaze, feeling like a cat stretched out in a sunbeam.

"That was comfort food," he said, "like potato soup. Reminds me of the afternoon my mama was sick and sent me to the store for bread and peanut butter."

She nodded.

"It's a long story," he said.

She closed her eyes. "I'm not going anywhere."

"Well, Mama handed me a twenty-dollar bill. 'Eddie,' she said, 'you're old enough to trust. Need you to run to the market.' I folded the money and put it deep in my jeans pocket. We didn't have many twenty-dollar bills in my house, you understand."

She smiled, feeling sleepy and soothed by the rhythm of his voice, so different from his barking out questions and facts in short bursts. "Go on."

"Pulling my red wagon, I walked the four blocks to Inks Brothers Market and picked a loaf of Sunbeam Bread off the shelf. I liked the little girl with blond ringlets on the wrapper. Then I lifted up a jar of Skippy Peanut Butter, the smooth kind my little brothers liked best, and put it in the wagon next to the bread. When I got up to the counter, I fished in my pocket for the twenty, but couldn't feel it. I shoved my hand deeper into the slot of the pocket, grabbed near the bottom, and yanked it inside out. Three puree marbles bounced out onto the floor, but there was nothing else in my pocket but some lint. Mr. Taylor frowned down from his post at the cash register. My heart started banging against my ribs.

'I had a twenty here when I started out,' I stammered, feeling around in the other pocket and then in the back ones, too, plus that little one in front for change. 'I know I had it when I started out,' I said. Mr. Taylor came around the counter and lifted the bread and peanut butter out of the wagon. 'Go on, son. Go on back and look for your money. I'll save these here for you.'"

"Sounds like the pressure of a deadline," Hillary said, feeling a bond with this man she barely knew. "Go on." She watched him. *Eddie,* she thought, *his mother called him Eddie.*

"Pulling the empty wagon behind, I walked back the exact same way I'd come, but no money lay on the sidewalk. I must have redone that trip a dozen times that day and more as the years went by, but never found the twenty. The worst part was that Mama didn't even get mad. She just hugged me and said we would have potato soup instead."

"Wow. That's what I wanted to make, but I didn't have any potatoes," Hillary said. "Comfort food." They looked at each other, wide-eyed. She felt like a child after one of Daddy's home-cooked-out-of-cans meals. Secure. Strong.

"Anyway," he said, "those twenties on Brookfield's desk that first morning made me think of that story. What do you make of them being twenties?"

A surge of energy hit her. "Something about prices, for sure, but this is no way to send a message. This crazy killer has got to be—" A sudden knocking at the door startled her. She stood and walked over to open the door to the guy who waited on Jacki and her at the country club.

"Hello, Ma'am. I was to meet Detective Kiffin here. I'm Matt, part-time waiter and part-time AJ student."

Images of favorite students at the college flashed to her mind, along with her methods to put up emotional walls, since sexual harassment went both ways nowadays. His nostrils flared as he inhaled the fried hash smell hanging in the air. "What have you been feeding our lawman?"

She waved the young man in. "It's unbelievable how this madman is hacking up PriceCuts' honchos—you going to help catch him?" Hillary sat back down to polish off the last crumbs of hash on her plate, wondering if she should open another can.

Ed's cell buzzed and he took the call, not saying much, just nodding, then flipping the phone closed.

"Got to go. Thanks for the hash—and for listening. Come on, youngster." He nodded at Matt then turned to Hillary. "Be sure to cover up all your windows!"

She bobbed her head and walked them to the door, more fearful than she'd been before about the peeper, who might be the cut-em-up killer.

"We'll get this monster. Promise." Ed gave her a squeeze on the arm and was gone.

She walked to the kitchen, ignoring the tears slipping down her cheeks. She wished she were back in New York, with her old troubles instead of this new set where everything seemed in danger of getting chopped into pieces. She rummaged through the cupboard. Nothing looked good. *How can I still be hungry? Eddie,* she thought, *his mother called him Eddie.* Her hunger intensified.

TWENTY-ONE

A Rehash

"HERE'S WHERE WE LOSE CONTROL," Ed whispered to Walt.

"We've got to coordinate this case, put it front and center," Sheriff Coats bellowed, seated at the far end of the conference table, and stating the obvious, as usual. Two FBI agents sat to his left. To his right, two Stockton police detectives, with Walt and Ed at the far end nearest the white boards on the wall.

"Our efforts are too scattered. The community needs us to go all out to find this madman," the sheriff continued. He glared at Ed.

Ed studied the elected law officer for a moment. It was common knowledge that Trevor Coats had ambitions to become attorney general—then governor or even higher. He was young and smart and knew that getting crimes like this solved, and fast, was essential to move him up the political ladder. He was into proving he could bring agencies together and get the job done.

"So what do we know for sure?" Ed asked, glancing at each man around the table. He felt humiliated that guys from the Stockton police had been added by the sheriff. Got to get this solved, him and Walt. "Two dead bodies, mutilated neatly, both found in the PriceCuts store here in San Joaquin County, just outside Clearwater, a week apart. Do we have a serial killer? Could this have anything to do with the Lodi ice cream vendor family and terrorist activities?" He didn't think so but wondered about the Pakistani optician Zasimo.

"It's unclear." Walt popped a couple peppermints into his mouth, snapped the tin shut, and slid it into his breast pocket.

"Is it possible the first was a decoy for the latter one?" Trevor Coats raised his eyebrows and flashed a bright white smile. "To hide it? Let's do some creative thinking here. I want this killer behind bars and fast."

Ed walked to the front of the room and uncapped a black dry erase marker. The sheriff didn't know what he was talking about. Onto the left side of a big whiteboard, under the heading BROOKFIELD, he listed the facts of the case in block printing, explaining as he went along.

"Monday, October 16, 7:58 a.m. Body number one—Steven Brookfield—discovered in Brookfield's office, head and arms severed cleanly, arms set into a design on the desk, trunk with legs attached sitting in the desk chair. Head missing. Time of death about 2:00 a.m. Monday. Sunday night and early Monday morning are busy as far as employee activity, unloading trucks and stocking product for opening time. The store closes to the public at midnight. Could have been either an employee or an outsider who snuck in. Nothing suspicious on the retail floor cameras, and no cameras in the backstore at that time."

Ed stepped to the far right side of the board and started listing facts under the STONEY heading.

"Monday morning, October 23, 7:51 a.m. Body number two—John Stoney—discovered in the Home Design Center. This victim also killed during the night around 2:00 a.m. The heart removed, the dismembered body moved from the kill site, going by the hypostasis pattern, body parts covered up by curtains used to conceal the new Design Center from public view until the opening, scheduled for eight that morning. Again, fastidious cutting of parts."

In a middle column, Ed began to list the commonalities. "No fingerprints other than the store employees, who would have been in and out in the normal run of their work. Either an inside job or the killer wore gloves."

He looked at the silent faces of the men sitting around the table, and seeing no objections, went on. "The manner of separation of body parts was proficient, clean, no blood found at either scene." He lifted the two preliminary autopsy reports and waved them as if to back up his statements. "Medical Examiner says asphyxiation caused both deaths, some kind of binding around the trunks and necks, going by what remains of the necks. All cutting was post mortem, after the blood settled, clean edges."

"We are looking at someone medically trained or a butcher or . . ." He turned to face the FBI agents. "Who else?"

"Hunters? Taxidermists?" Voices chimed in for ten minutes or so as men took notes. No one seemed to agree on a focus.

The sheriff brought the session to a close by urging the men to work together. Ed felt justified they had produced little in the way of new direction. This was a tough case, not to be solved with a snap of the fingers. The FBI guys planned to dig into the Lodi terrorist connection possibilities, but Ed thought that a dim prospect.

Finding the peeper seemed more productive to him, along with following up on the designs the parts were laid out in. He had Mendoza working on a mockup of each of the two body part layouts, but the two seemed to have very little in common except that both had some fingers cut off. One head missing, one heart missing—what kind of message was the killer trying to send? Ed thought of the 4H club for kids who lived in rural settings. What did it stand for? Head, heart, hands…? Did that fit?

Part of Ed's job was to keep Trevor Coats satisfied they were working the case hard. At least they'd accomplished that, but they weren't meeting up with success yet. Success—the elusive achievement Ed ached for, in more ways than one.

TWENTY-TWO

A Few Finds

IN PURSUIT OF A FOLLOW-UP STORY, Hillary reached the PriceCuts general manager by phone and found out he was trying to pull strings with the sheriff to get the superstore reopened fast, get the Jacki Jones event rescheduled. It was taking too damn much time for investigators to finish working the scene. He hung up in a huff.

Ed called a second later, and after getting her to agree to keep it off the record, divulged what his team had discovered on a bottom shelf in the Pharmacy department. It was a wig, a curly salt and pepper wig tucked behind the Epsom salts. His voice transmitted his elation. She was impressed about this find moving the investigation although frustrated to learn it could take weeks before the DNA folks could process it, they were so backed up. It gave her the creeps every time she entered PriceCuts to work on the story. So far, no contact from Charles, though. She felt whipsawed between fear and relief.

* * *

The next day, customers flocked into the store at the noon re-opening, although the Design Center remained closed off—this time with plywood instead of sheeting—until Jacki's people could get it cleaned up and reconfigured.

Hillary interviewed Jacki in the white conference room behind Brookfield's office, now being used as a workroom for the Design Center's postponed opening. Jacki and the PriceCuts higher-ups had agreed to remodel the demonstration kitchen area completely so the location of Stoney's cut-up body was obliterated and replaced with a bathroom in a lavish style, aligned with the nesting trend still popular after 9/11. People wanted to make their homes inviting places of safety. Jacki was still determined to put a positive spin on what looked like a serial killer on the loose with a grudge against PriceCuts' managers, and Hillary felt grateful the sophisticated woman was giving her exclusive interviews.

Today, Hillary set aside her notebook and let her tape recorder pick up most of the information. Jacki chattered on with her rah-rah about how much PriceCuts helped the community with programs like interior design internships for the nearby community colleges. Hillary made a mental note for a follow-up story opportunity to suggest for her journalism students.

Jacki shifted topics to her hiring a crew out of San Francisco to ramp up the condition of the place for public viewing. The official opening of the JJL Design Center was rescheduled for the following Tuesday, since Monday had become a bad luck day. "Cut rate Mondays" the Inquirer was calling it and that had caught on with major media. The public seemed more eager than ever to spill into the store, despite two killings in a week's time—or perhaps because of them. But the key question, Jacki said, was whether they would buy or only come to gawk at the notorious site and shuffle around, hoping to get interviewed or show up in a video clip to grab their fifteen minutes of fame, or what few minutes of it were possible.

Jacki said that GM Ron Tompkins had held a general staff alert, calling employees and independent contractors alike into the conference room, warning them to be watchful for anything suspicious, any odd behavior from customers, or from other staffers. They were all directed to be on the lookout, especially for body parts. With a leer, Jacki went on to report that Tompkins had vigorously denied the rumor that a shriveled penis had been found plastic wrapped onto a package of pork sausages.

Called "associates" at PriceCuts, the staffers for the most part had laughed and made jokes in the meeting, Jacki said, especially the kitchenware staff, sellers of all sorts of knives. The hardware department employees were more serious about their saws and pruning shears. And the butchers stood frozen faced at the discussion.

Jacki asked Hillary to come by the store often and check out the shelves, let her know first if she found any body parts. Hillary agreed, and got into a habit of walking the long aisles, thinking of the distances as in a way replacing her jogs through Morada. This wasn't the time to focus on losing weight.

* * *

Hillary attended the press conferences Ed and his staff held for the media. They cautioned all reporters to observe, not to touch or try doing anything but simply report suspicious objects or behavior. Ed offered a mnemonic device—STOP

KILLS—so everyone would have the hotline phone number memorized. Hillary felt proud to have Ed's private cell number as well. She found her respect for him growing day by day—along with her attraction to the slim, intense detective, who'd shared some of the agony of his daughter's death and the fallout with his wife and other daughter in the year to follow. He was alone now, same as she was.

* * *

Hillary was amazed that the extreme dismemberments had not kept shoppers away. Most people didn't know the killer had left some body parts unaccounted for. She wondered if that knowledge would draw in fewer customers, or more.

PriceCuts' loss leaders were at an all time high. Savvy customers from as far away as Monterey and northeast up to Reno flocked in for the hourly announcements of items on seventy-five percent off sale An ad campaign through the Jacki Jones JJL website to decorate for Christmas was pulling in business like crazy, too. Not to mention the new PriceCuts credit card savings, linked up to super easy-to-get Home Equity credit lines. This 2005 economy was hot and getting hotter.

* * *

Hillary walked though and scanned store aisles every time she had a spare hour. Ed wanted her on the lookout for index and pinkie fingers, particularly.

This afternoon, she glanced at displays of Thanksgiving cornucopia centerpieces. Alongside brown and purple Indian corn and yellow crookneck squash laid out on an eye-level shelf, she spotted an odd-looking orb huddled up next to a bunch of Thompson seedless grapes. She peered at the irregular piece—pale and wrinkled. She glanced back and forth from it to the grapes. *Holy Mary.*

She didn't want to touch it. Wasn't supposed to anyway. This killer was carving a new section in Dante's Inferno—she wondered who he considered the sinners? It was horrible to leave bodies cut up in the store. But to take parts to scatter later, diabolical. Her stomach churned. *Thank God I found this and not a customer. Maybe it's only an odd grape.*

She backed away and punched in STOP KILLS.

Ed answered.

"I think I found something on the Thanksgiving shelf in Aisle 49," Hillary muttered. Horrified, she suddenly wanted to angle her coverage in defense of PriceCuts, to combat this fiend trying to drive away customers. It was a new kind of terror, subtle and powerful.

"I'll be right over," Ed said. "Do not put that into a story, promise me. Got to keep it as the kind of detail only the killer knows."

If it really is an eyeball, she thought. She wandered around the Thanksgiving shelves, searching for more of what she hoped not to find. She had lost all her enthusiasm for the fall season.

TWENTY-THREE

A House Call

THE NEXT DAY, HILLARY walked by the Spectacular Eyes optical alcove in the front of the store and noticed Dr. Zasimo measuring an old man for glasses. *Has Ed fully investigated him?*

She went to the backstore conference room to question Jacki. "Do you know anything about that doctor in eye exams?" she asked.

"Haven't a clue." Jacki was rewriting the script for her TV promo, scheduled for noon the next day. "Why?"

"I wondered what he might be capable of. Ed said they cleared him, but that doctor—I think he's Muslim—could be outraged about the way meat gets handled here. I've researched the halal process of slaughtering animals for food, and I know that's not the way PriceCuts meat is butchered, for sure. Just wondering if this could fit into a jihad against the American way."

"I don't know about that, sweetie. You better run that by the detectives. All I know is, despite the pain in the butt of rebuilding this JJL Center, there's no such thing as bad PR." Jacki grinned. "Our consumer ratings are way up now, nationwide and even international, going by the website traffic."

"You didn't put out the hits yourself, for the publicity, did you?" Hillary teased, looking at Jacki, who smiled back.

"Wouldn't want to go to prison all that long, sweetie face."

* * *

Hillary got on the phone to Ed and wheedled Dr. Zasimo's address out of him after she promised to focus on general interest, approach him as part of gathering reactions from a range of PriceCuts staffers. From her research into the terrorist angle, she knew this was the season of Ramadan, so she waited until sundown to go call at the doctor's apartment address and see what she could learn.

She parked half a block away, so as to not announce her arrival in case he wanted to ignore her. After walking uphill in semi-darkness, she knocked on his apartment door. She listened but couldn't hear anything. He probably wouldn't answer. She waited a few beats, knocked again, and was surprised to find the door opened by the doctor himself, wearing a sort of embroidered dressing gown.

"Hello. I'm Hillary Broome from the newspaper in town." She gestured in the direction of the office. "I've come to warn you, Dr. Zasimo."

His eyebrows shot up, but he was polite. "Come in. Please." He bent at the waist and waved her into the apartment.

He motioned her through a dim living room into a kitchen painted bright yellow and pulled out a chair at a table set for two. Hillary sat, enjoying the fragrances of Middle Eastern food she'd eaten in New York. "Meet Hayaam, my wife." He nodded toward a woman working at the stove.

Unveiled, the attractive woman looked over without comment, added a third plate, and served her husband nan with butter and honey, yogurt, and a small wedge of halva shekari, along with hot coffee.

"We eat simply in this time." She glanced at Hillary, poured her some coffee, and sat down, angled toward the side a bit, to accommodate her obvious pregnancy.

The doctor clamped his thick lips around a piece of crumbly brown and tan halva, chewed on the ground sesame sweet, and swallowed. "You say you have come to warn me?"

Hillary took a sip of the thick coffee, swallowing her guilt at breaking her promise to Ed. "Some of the law think you might be a suspect in the killings at the store." She wanted to see Zasimo's reaction.

Hayaam made no comment but poured her husband a refill of coffee with graceful motions, the barest of smiles on her shapely lips. She did not look at her husband.

"She carries my son now, Praise be to God, and they need to be protected." He finished his small meal in silence, rose from the table, and pointed to the front room. "I want you to hear my story."

He waited until Hillary was comfortably seated and then he began.

"I came ten years ago, hoping to work as an eye surgeon, but learned my medical school was not recognized here. I could only get the optometrist certification, so far, same as my brother. We are naturalized Americans, five years ago. We have been quiet during the ice cream vendor and son investigation, trying to show ourselves good citizens. We don't like rocks turned over on our community and insults piled on the humble Lodi mosque. Most of us go elsewhere to pray on Fridays."

Hillary was taking mental notes.

"Despite the evils I see all around me, I would not kill now of all times. For years we saw no blessings and then, last summer . . ." He wiped his forehead with a white handkerchief and folded it into a triangle. "She never complained." He closed his eyes and swayed in his chair. "Killing and going to prison is the last thing I would do, although I rejoice when I see infidels suffer. Allahu Akbar!" He rose and walked to his front door. "Thank you for hearing me out."

Hillary left, thinking his dignity was puzzling and on the unconvincing side, but unsure what to do with his side of the story.

TWENTY-FOUR

A Different Lesson

HILLARY GREETED HER STUDENTS by reading Brookfield's obituary aloud, in which the memorial service was called a party, following the widow's request.

"There will be a crowd," she said, loving their rapt attention. "And the public is invited." Her stock with them had risen considerably since she'd witnessed both cases of dramatic news first hand. "This will be quite the unique event for you to cover."

She encouraged the students to surf the Internet for background matter on the famous couple. As they hunted, the students shouted out into the room the interesting bits they discovered. With her union to Steven Brookfield, Belinda was on her seventh marriage. "Lucky number seven" she was quoted in one blog. The aging star who came across as a Southern Belle from ages ago had not appeared in a film for over a decade, but lived on ego gratification from her half dozen minor roles in the 80s. Speculation over what she saw in Brookfield was the theme for tabloid articles in the months before his murder, and had been ramped up tenfold since. In the opinion of many snoops, linking up with an ordinary guy who managed PriceCuts human resources never seemed enough reason for marriage.

The rumors ended up being the truth, as the budding journalists learned that evening in their online searching. Brookfield was a closet bisexual, as Hillary already knew—not public in so many words, but people with every sort of sexual preference and identity were now known to have attended his parties.

"Look at this." Hillary read out bits from her online findings as she scrolled the articles. "From his resume and our initial reference checks, he had an upright background," PriceCuts Board Chairman William Hatcher was quoted.

"We ourselves have no proof otherwise. In the American tradition, Brookfield was an innocent victim," said the other Hatcher brother, Dennis. The students noted that the giant corporation appeared sympathetic to Brookfield or at least not hostile.

"Guess it's fitting that the memorial shindig's at night." Hillary rolled her eyes at the students. "It's on Halloween—there should be costumes worth a look-see, at least 'R' rated, I'm thinking."

The young writers were abuzz and speculated whether the killer would show up. The copy editor wondered if any of the local Muslim community would be scoping out the place. Hillary tried to downplay those edgy aspects but they bubbled with energy over it. Very seldom did anyone get to cover a story this bizarre in their little town. Hillary prayed it wouldn't get any stranger.

TWENTY-FIVE

A Cold Room

ON WEDNESDAY AFTERNOON, Hillary stopped by PriceCuts to do her usual body-parts check and strolled around in the meat section. A guy dressed in a white coat smudged with a few blood smears pushed a stainless steel cart loaded with cuts of meat down the aisle. He flashed her a bright smile.

"How about these tonight?" He held up some beef filets, packed into what looked like clear plastic jumbo-sized muffin tins. Each of the cups was lined with bacon strips wrapped around the filet so all that showed of the beef was a deep red circle on the bottom. "Can you believe it?" He waved the meat around in the air. "Make them back in the Midwest and cold ship 'em here by rail. Call 'em aged."

"They look tender," Hillary said. She saw a lot of white marbling. Fat. *What I should not be eating.*

"Less cutting on site, nowadays. Tell us we should be grateful." He grinned wide, as if posing for a dentist's ad. "Only have to cut up 'bout half the meat ourselves, lucky us back in Deli and meat." He bent down to transfer blister packs into the refrigerated meat case and loaded the white enamel bin full, plus stacked a few layers above the top. "Got to move the meat."

Within a minute or two, he had cleared off his cart and rolled it empty back toward a set of metal doors through which he disappeared, leaving the two vertical halves banging back and forth, like doors to a saloon in an old Western movie.

An intuition compelled Hillary to follow him. "Excuse me!" she yelled, trying to get his attention. She pushed the doors open and went down an alleyway that snaked through stacks of cardboard boxes. The maze reminded her of an old urban legend where two brothers were found dead in a houseful of newspapers piled up to the ceilings.

It was cold, and she wondered if it was all right for her to be there. She looked around for security cameras but spotted none.

She repeated a mantra teachers at the college said they used when in tricky situations: It's better to ask forgiveness than permission. She could hear from the cart wheels that the butcher was moving in the direction of a frosty, white space. She shivered but kept going.

The dim cool pathway opened onto a large room that held half a dozen stainless steel tables. Rubber hoses hung above the tables, which looked more like huge sinks as she got closer. There were drains in the ends of each metal sink, with men standing at the tables, pulling frozen meat from nearby cardboard boxes and hoisting the cold carcasses up and over, into the sinks. They were spraying the meat with water then yanking saws on pulleys down from the ceiling.

Hillary stood stock still, mouth agape, as the men cut hunks of meat into smaller chunks, then threw them onto moving assembly belts which whisked them away, out of this neon lit room. She was fascinated and fearful at the same time. No one seemed to have noticed her.

The man she'd followed had disappeared. She backed up soundlessly, retreating until she found the swinging doors she'd come in through, and pushed her way back onto the retail floor. Had to ask Ed if they'd investigated that butchering operation in the backstore.

TWENTY-SIX

Indignation

I THREW *THE ACORN* into the trash. Damn that Hillary Broome! And all those other reporters, swarming the place, writing about PriceCuts' rights to build here and do business as they please. Property rights! Wrong, wrong, wrong.

In the dim kitchen, I rocked in Mother's chair. She'd rocked me in this until I was five and would have gone on longer but that neighbor kid Buck told his mother I was a sugar-tit ninny, so Mother quit. Cared too much about what others thought.

I sat here over the past year, trying to figure out what went wrong. It would have been better if we kept up our protests. If only I'd joined in, but it seemed unprofessional. Instead, I'd taken lunches to the picketers along the roadside when PriceCuts Phase I was being built. Lean beef on French rolls, buckets of barbecued chicken and ribs. By the last few weeks of construction, the demonstrators had turned dusty and discouraged.

"It's a hopeless cause," Jimmy Hubbard sighed. "We're too late. Should'a got on this when the environmental impact study was done, back then in the planning process." His family had run Clearwater Ladies' Apparel since the end of the Depression.

"Never thought it'd get this far. Them greedy bastards." Hans Schmiedt nodded as he reached for his third drumstick. "Melvin, they can't run you out of business, not with what you and John do for the town."

149

I had smiled at that, ignorant fool that I was. I never imagined Stoney's customers would desert us for a few dollars savings.

* * *

My comfort movie formed in my mind. Mother was singing to me in the bathtub. "Rub-a-dub-dub, three men in the tub and who do you think they are? The butcher, the baker, the candlestick maaaaaaaaaker—that's who they are."

"And the butcher is at the top," she used to squeal, laughing and squeezing a sponge over my head so the warm bubbles swirled down over my black curls. She would wrap me tight in a fluffy white towel, blot me all over, and dress me with care, then we would walk downtown to Stoney's to watch Father slice meat ever so neatly, with his long slim boning knife.

* * *

I walked to the entry hall mirror and ran my hand back off my forehead to smooth the short bristles. Even as a child, I was squat and dark-haired. Before I turned three, my twin brother—five minutes older than I and not identical—had died of a rare blood cancer, and Mother had shifted onto me the role of taking up our father's butchering trade. As soon as PriceCuts opened its doors in Phase I, before they even added a meat and fresh food section, damned if it wasn't flooded with customers, like a flock of geese turned off their migration route and lured into a field of new grain. I began to lose hope then, but wouldn't utter my fears to John, not to Sarah either.

If I voiced it, it might come to pass. It would all be over for me if we lost Stoney's and the meat shop.

My face in the mirror looked somber as a death mask. As soon as PriceCuts started hiring for Phase II's addition of meat and fresh food to the huge retail outlet, John started acting funny. Near the end, he even brought Steven Brookfield into our place to try and recruit me. The nerve.

It wasn't only John's fault, though. Sarah should have made John stand up, like Mother made Father strong during the mad cow scare, another time folks had stopped buying. We came through that just fine. Mother was a survivor. Not Sarah.

I'd taken the PriceCuts job to get inside, see what was going on and figure out how to cut down the giant. Like David and Goliath. The shepherd boy had his slings and stones, I had my bungees and knives.

But people weren't getting the message. Unbelievable.

Customers were flocking to PriceCuts, more now than ever—damn greedy short-sighted whackos— wanting to see for themselves, see and be seen—the numbers were way up in the daytime when folks thought they were safe. I felt a stab of triumph over the fact that fewer customers shopped late anymore—the two night killings had completed part of my work to cut down the giant.

I had to move the location, block the passion of defending PriceCuts business "rights." Security was all over the whole building. How could I pull it off somewhere else and still make the PriceCuts connection? One or two kills off site, reach out into the community, make shoppers reconsider the consequences of their actions, cut down the volume of day sales—at the same time, force the greedy bastards to rethink coming into our town and taking over.

They weren't immune to having to close up shop themselves, though they sure thought they were.

It was a matter of tradition, of family values. I sat rocking in the chair she'd held me in over the years, watching movies in my mind as I thought about ways to bring back our small shops. I rocked and hummed "Rub-a-dub-dub," one note at a time, the way she used to.

TWENTY-SEVEN

A Memorial Party

HILLARY THOUGHT IT ODD that Halloween fell on Monday, precisely two weeks after the Brookfield killing. The "memorial party," as the Funeral Notice called it, was to start soon, at six in the evening. Daylight Savings time was over. It was dark except for the glow of a bright half-moon. Morada was creepy at night with its thick groves of trees and twisting pathways. She felt alone and powerless.

Waiting for Roger to come so they could walk together to the memorial, she leaned against the cottage wall and stared at the three English walnut trees in her side yard, a trinity of thick gray trunks, spliced onto black walnut bases decades ago, among the few left standing from the hundreds planted in Morada's orchards. They exuded strength. She pushed out her belly to inhale deep, relishing the earthy smell that carried memories of the walnut tree in the backyard of her childhood. After he cracked the wrinkly shells open, Daddy would let her pick the fresh nutmeats out, their pungent fragrance a treat in her small hands. Even so, these trees in Morada could be providing cover for someone far from fatherly. She shuddered.

She went inside to recheck the window locks, feeling more vulnerable to the peeper now that it got dark early. *Why can't Ed catch him and arrest him— put him behind bars and see if the carnage stops or continues.*

The brass knocker thudded at the door. After looking through the peephole, she let Roger in.

"Ready to go trick or treating?" He motioned her outside. "See what haul we can come home with."

"Hope it's not razor blades in our candy." She laughed without joy.

On the road, TV vans were parked facing the Brookfield mansion. The center of the road become a narrow passageway through vehicles parked on both sides. Hillary and Roger joined the parade snaking along the country lane, a march of figures in soft moonlight. The mansion gate was open and they fell in with the stream of people threading up the front steps and through the entry hall.

Belinda stood halfway up the curving white staircase, dressed in a black silk gown that clung to her curves but showed no cleavage. She wore a black lace veil covering her hair and secured with combs in a sort of mantilla look.

"The grieving widow," Roger muttered.

Not until she descended and strode into the living room for the start of the service did anyone see the butt-crack-revealing backside of Belinda's outfit. A low gasp from the mourners was silenced when she pivoted mid-way up the aisle formed between rows of folding chairs. She smiled wide and bright like a Cheshire cat, then turned to slink up to her seat in front. A podium—flanked by spikes of corn stalks sprayed silver in tall black urns—stood at attention before the massive fireplace.

"Let's see if we can weave Belinda's use of local materials to achieve a somber tone into our story," Roger whispered to Hillary. "The contrasting black and silver—perfect."

"Will do," she agreed. The place looked theatrical, like a stage set.

154

"And," he continued, rotating his head and nodding toward the windows at the room's perimeter, "you don't see that anymore, draping windows with black crepe. It used to be to keep the sun out before the days of refrigeration."

"Thank God there is no coffin . . ."

"Don't remind me of the condition his beautiful body ended up in." Roger's eyes took on a steely glare. "Thankfully, he's been cremated." He nodded at a silver urn on the mantle. Recorded music swelled into the room from hidden speakers.

"God, I can't believe it." Roger pulled out a handkerchief from his breast pocket and wiped his mouth.

Belinda began to nod her head and upper torso to a familiar rhythm.

Hillary couldn't place the music but it had a distinct pulse to it, and she frowned at Roger.

"It's from an old film, *The Stripper*," whispered Roger. "The one she credits with motivating her career. They used to play it in the San Francisco bathhouses. In the old days."

Others began moving to the seductive beat. As the piece concluded, Belinda stood and walked the few steps to the podium.

"Thank you for coming to celebrate Steven's life." Her voice rang out strong and clear. "He would have wanted this party, finally to show his true nature, to be out of that miserable closet our hypocritical culture nailed him into. He was the best, a lover of freedom and pleasure. I celebrated his life this past week in Mexico with the healing hands of Carlos, Steven's favorite masseuse, who would sooth away his nerves stretched taut by the pressure of the business world."

Lavender eyes flashing, she motioned toward a dark-skinned man standing a few feet from her, dressed in Aztec garb complete with feathered headdress and seed pod leggings. Scowling, he nodded to the crowd as the sounds of soft drumming built in the room.

"In Steven's memory, celebrating what would have been our second wedding anniversary, and in the spirit of Dia de los Muertos coming up soon, I offer you all a cup of kindness." Belinda waited, nodding at individuals in the front rows while silver trays of champagne were passed along the rows.

"On this All Hallows Eve, I invite you to create a costume from our supplies out near the pool." She waved in the direction of the French doors, open to the patio and pool beyond. "Put on the look of your true being, free from convention, if only for this one night—trick the world and treat yourself. The most creative costume will win the first annual Steven Brookfield Memorial Prize. Let's celebrate life!"

She took a glass of champagne from a tray, raised it in the direction of the silver urn on the fireplace mantel. "Yesterday, today, and tomorrow, Steven, you are missed and remembered."

"Remembered," echoed Roger morosely.

Hillary spotted lawmen in the crowd. Ed leaned against the front wall of the room. She sipped at her bubbling drink and studied his grim face as he stood next to one of the black crepe swags, draped over a window and falling to the floor. Walt was not three feet from him, both detectives blending into the crowd except for their narrowed eyes, the eyes of hunters.

"Will the killer show up at this party?" A gravelly voice sung out from behind her.

She looked over her shoulder. Clarice sat next to some co-workers from PriceCuts. Nodding at her, Hillary muttered to Roger, "Let's see if we can spot a murderer in the crowd."

Belinda had stepped away from the podium, leaving her formally dressed butler at attention in front of the silver urn. The music shifted to jazz. People stood in place and snapped their fingers to the rhythms, waiting for those at the ends of rows to move out the back doors. It was dark but still warm outside. Despite the rain last week, the weather held the heat of Indian summer days like it did most years before the first true cold snap in the Central Valley would signal leaves to start falling.

Hillary and Roger walked out to see racks of costumes set out beyond the swimming pool, which shimmered with aqua ripples from mini-waterfalls pouring into the water. Trays of champagne stood every ten feet along with platters of prawns, stuffed mushrooms, black caviar and water crackers, ripe brie and sliced baguettes.

Hillary peered at a tray of small sausages wrapped in dough, all brown and sizzling. No, can't be. One of the sausages looked suspicious, the way the wrinkling was formed, not unlike a fingertip left soaking in a tub too long. *Holy Mary.* She took it and wrapped it in a black paper napkin to give Ed. Had the killer sneaked this in? Was he here?

"It's unreal." She surveyed the crowd. "Looks like Mardi Gras."

Roger laughed. "This is every day and night down in the City Steven loved." He nodded to a couple dressed in matching red satin dresses, one with coal black hair flowing down past buttocks rounded into the shape of bowls, the other whose head was shaved bald. "Those two drove up. You should see them at Gay Pride parades."

"Wonder if the peeper came?" She looked over toward the vine-clad fence.

"Have to go check it out. Got to be awful sick to peep when he could be in here as a guest, like the rest of us." Roger moved in the direction of the pool, ignoring the faint sounds of chanting coming from the front of the mansion. "Want to trick or treat?" He leered at her.

"The killer could be right here," she muttered.

"Our sheriff friends are casing the joint with their FBI pals, relax." Roger nodded in the direction of the pool. "Come on."

Just then, she bumped into a man backing away from the crowd. "Sorry," she murmured.

He turned around, waving a pair of warty rubber gloves in front of his chest, like a misshapen pair of breasts on some ancient hag. "What a way to memorialize a husband," the man said. He shook the rubber hands once more and threw them back onto a canvas cart.

"Yeah, toward the perverted side, as memorials go," she agreed, trying to recall if she'd seen the man before.

Roger busied himself taking digital shots. They had worried that Belinda would not allow photos, but there didn't seem to be prohibitions of any kind here.

"She might have killed Steven herself just for the excuse to hold this wild party," a thin woman exclaimed, wrinkling her nose with disgust.

Others were pawing through the cart, pulling out plastic whole-head masks with bloody neck stumps, sawn off empty feet, and rubber hands, fingers dangling like claws, some with hair sprouting out the top.

"I wouldn't put on any of this if you paid me," said a man in a Pendleton shirt and Levi's.

Roger came back from a nearby rack of costumes, waving around a tuxedo. The bow tie at the top was undone and the pants were cut off at the knees. "Here's a little more traditional outfit, like what Grandfather would have approved." He thrust the black and white tux at Hillary.

She tossed it in the Pendleton man's direction. He grabbed it and threw it with force into the swimming pool. "Too much. I'm out of here." He melted back into the crowd, and she lost track of him.

* * *

Chanting from the front of the mansion took on meaning as it grew in volume. "Sodom burned with sulfur and fire, and you will along with it! Repent."

"Come on." Hillary grabbed Roger's arm. They slipped past the crowd pawing through costumes at the poolside and moved over near the darkness of the fence. They edged toward the front of the mansion, staying near the fence wall to avoid the religious fanatics clustered at the entry steps. Hillary studied the fence.

"Look for the peeper," she whispered.

They peered into the night, straining to see an opening in the greenery or a head at the top of the property perimeter. Nothing. She rounded the corner, hoping to pass behind the demonstrators and out the front gate.

* * *

"No one escapes the wrath of the Lord." A second wave of protesters pushed into the mansion yard, headed by a wiry young man. He screamed at them, waving a sign by its wooden handle, thrusting it up and down. "The wages of sin are death!" scrawled his message in thick and curvy Germanic script.

"Get back home, young woman." He stared at Hillary for a second, and then, along with his fellow zealots, passed on by toward the open front door of the mansion. "Go. And don't look back," were his last shouted words before he disappeared into the mansion's mob scene.

Hillary looked over at Roger. "Did you get pictures?"

"Foul cretins." He nodded, scowling. "Right or wrong. Gay or straight—no complexity in their simple-minded world."

He looked straight into her eyes. "Steven despised this kind of hostility. It could have been a hate crime pure and simple, and Stoney's killing just to throw the cops off."

They left the party and headed for *The Acorn* office, eager to get the dazzling event posted up on their website and into print for the morning special edition. Hillary knew Roger might have captured the killer's face in the photos. But how would they recognize him?

TWENTY-EIGHT

A Brush-Off

DREAMS OF WITCHES pushing straw brooms across alleys paved with gravel disturbed Hillary's sleep. She woke mulling over last night's memorial scene and set out for a run through Morada, its shadows long in the early morning sunlight. She carried her pepper spray. Living here in the forest, she was feeling more sensitive to mystical forces. The notion of ley lines came to mind, places of magical power on the planet she'd heard of over the years but never experienced before. An energy streamed into her bones as she ran, not needing to slow to a walk today.

What's going on here? What compels the killer? Killers? What drives these flatland customers? He wants to impress them or what? She felt conflicted over the shoppers. They aren't any different from other people, she lectured herself. Just want to save money. They aren't greedy-guts supporting a global business model—they are people the same as my students and me.

Within forty-five minutes, she'd covered the three miles of winding roads that made up Morada. Today she and Roger were taking a day off, having a leisurely lunch at her place. Circling back toward the cottage, she passed by Belinda Brookfield's where Ed and Walt's unmarked was parked outside along with several media vans still there.

A figure halfway down the estate fence line turned to face her, stepped down off something, and strode in her direction through damp walnut

161

leaves, stirring up the fragrance of fall that she loved. It was the cute young waiter. Matt.

"What's up?" She sucked in her stomach, wiped the sweat off her temples and ran her hands over her hair, trying to smooth it.

"On an early ride-along with Ed and Walt." He jerked his thumb toward an unmarked vehicle.

"What were you doing back there?"

"There's a couple self-inflating mattresses pushed up to the fence. We're investigating."

Her belly grew cold—the damn peeper. Last night even with Roger along, she hadn't let herself go outside the fence and look for the perch of the peeping Tom that Ed had warned her about. Did the peeper have other platforms?

Just then Ed and Walt came out through the Brookfield estate gate.

"Hey, Hillary," Ed said. "You remember Matt?"

She had to wall off herself off from her young journalism students, but she felt free to enjoy Matt's vitality.

"Thought of anything else out here in the woods?" Ed positioned his elbows on top of the unmarked, folded his long fingers together, and gazed over at her.

She shook her head, just as an image of the man in front of her at the guard station that first Monday popped to mind. Black rubber-soled shoes, an ashy substance caked around the edges of the soles, like what her Pumas picked up on her walks.

"It's probably nothing . . ."

Ed ran his fingers through his disheveled hair. Must not have time for a cut. "Anything could be worthwhile. We never know." It struck her how cute Ed was, in the way of a loveable pet, with his reddish brown hair flying free like an Irish setter's.

"Well, that guy in front of me at the guard desk the morning they found ..." She tipped her head toward the Brookfield estate. "Him. You know."

Ed and Walt nodded in unison.

"The guy in line had dirt on his shoes like I get on mine walking out here in the forest."

"The forest?" Ed raised his eyebrows.

"That's what I call this old orchard. Reminds me of the song 'Once upon a time in the black forest . . .'"

Matt began humming the simple melody.

"That's it," she shouted.

"About a ballerina and her toy soldier or something." He grinned and Hillary felt a warmth in her heart to think a young man would know something Donovan sang way back when she was a girl, happy at home with her parents, singing songs from the 60s.

"Yeah," she said, throwing her arms out in glee and feeling like giving him a big hug.

Ed cleared his throat and brought her back to the task of the moment.

"Anyway, when I moved into the cottage and started jogging through the forest," she smiled at Matt and waved her arm toward the lot that lay beyond the bend in the road, "I would get a sooty dirt on my shoes that was hard to clean off, so I wear these old things." She leaned against a tree and lifted one ankle onto the other thigh, so the three men could see the bottom of her shoe, with its black hobnail-style sole.

"Doesn't look much different from mine." Ed lifted one foot and inspected his sole that had been tramping over layers of leaf mold near the Brookfield place.

"It's different after you get past the lot with the ashes. Come see." She pulled at the edge of Ed's suit sleeve and started to run ahead down the road.

Walt and Matt followed behind in the unmarked sheriff's car.

She sprinted around the turn. When Ed caught up, she had tramped back and forth in front of an ashy pile of rubble.

"See?" She leaned against a walnut tree trunk and raised her left shoe high. "It's different now. Burnt ashes mixed with the dirt. That's what that man ahead of me in line had on the edges of his soles!"

Ed pulled out his cell phone, yanked it open, and punched in numbers. "Get CSI over here, take some soil samples," he barked. "West of the Brookfield place a couple hundred yards. It's the lot where you can see some kind of structure burnt to the ground."

Matt and Walt jumped out of the car. Hillary held up her shoe for them to take a look. Matt gave a low whistle. Walt frowned at his partner. "How about taking a look-see back in there?" He jerked his head toward the back of the lot. "Looks like a thicket beyond the ashes, with some kind of outbuildings, maybe."

Ed jumped into the unmarked and started the engine. "We can follow up later. Promised to have Matt over to the Academy for the start of class." Matt got into the back seat while Walt rode shotgun in front.

"Thanks, Hillary," Ed called out the window and they peeled off in their own dust cloud. Why was Ed was in such an all-fired hurry to get away?

She walked back toward the cottage, hungry for lunch.

TWENTY-NINE

A Shed

HILLARY STOPPED by Morada Market and picked up local produce for a spinach, apple and fennel salad. At home, she tossed it all together and covered the bowl to let the flavors mingle.

A little before noon, Roger arrived with marinated Cornish game hens and a couple bottles of Chardonnay. He placed the miniature chickens, cut into halves, on the outdoor grill. Within twenty minutes, they were eating the tasty hens along with focaccia bread dipped in olive oil and balsamic vinegar, plus Hillary's salad.

"What do you guess the widow woman's mansion will look like today?" She licked a residue of savory poultry skin off her fingers. The skin had always been her favorite part. *Got to give it up. All that fat.*

"Let's take some of our leftovers and wine down her way, be neighborly." He waggled his eyebrows. She felt relieved to have a somewhat normal day off to break the tension of the past few weeks.

"I'll put goodies in a basket—be Red Riding in the 'hood." She laughed. After wrapping up the food and grabbing a bottle of Chardonnay, she stuck it all into a picnic hamper and led the way out of the cottage, making sure to cover the windows and lock the door, as usual.

"Hoping for rain, get past any fire danger." Roger held out his hand, palm up to the sky, as if waiting for drops to appear. "It's predicted soon."

They trod the country lane, rounding the bend toward the estate. The iron gate came into view. Hillary had started to think of the place as a scaled-down Playboy Mansion in the forest.

"No perverts casing the joint today," Roger said as they passed the fence.

Hillary peered down the fence line. "Looks like CSIs have taken away the mattress, too. Maybe they'll put the peeper out of business, I hope."

They approached the front gate. Roger pressed the intercom button and waited. Nothing. He rang three more times. Still no response.

"Maybe the widow wants be left alone." He pulled out his cell phone and thumbed in a number.

Hillary raised her eyebrows. "Think she was here this morning. I came by on my run when Ed and Walt were just leaving."

Roger nodded. "Steven gave me the house phone number last year when we were getting reacquainted."

Her eyes widened.

"Let's see if he's still giving out their voice mail message or if she replaced it." He thumbed the Speaker On button.

"Darling, you know what to do after the beep, and I'll be sure to get back to you." Belinda's intimate tone invited a response.

Roger sighed and spoke into the phone. "Roger Ingram here, Belinda. We came by to see how you're doing. Call when you feel like visitors bearing gourmet leftovers. I do delicious with Cornish hens." He added a low chuckle to his message, gave his cell number and then punched the End button.

"I don't think she's a bad person," he said. "Just kind of screwed up. But who isn't, anymore." He shook his head.

Hillary gestured down the road past the mansion, toward the lot with the pile of ashes, wondering if the CSIs had been there yet. "On my run by here this morning," she said, "I talked to Ed and Walt." He raised his eyebrows.

She set down the picnic hamper, leaned against an ancient tree, and lifted her foot onto the opposite knee to expose the sole of her shoe. "See that ashy dirt in there?"

He bent down, looked and nodded. "Another mysterious fire in the old groves. Some dangerous folks out here." He frowned.

"It's kind of like what I saw the morning Brookfield's body was discovered."

"How so?"

"On the shoes of the guy ahead of me in line, before I went into the store. I showed Ed this morning, but he hasn't paid enough attention, if you ask me. Let's go over and poke around, see if we can find anything," she said.

"Lead the way, Riding Hood. Maybe there's a patio or something back there. We can drink wine in the forest while we cogitate."

They crossed to the other side of the road and walked for a few minutes. Hillary turned in perpendicular to the road, onto a vacant lot, which held what could have been a small house, lately transformed into a lumpy mound of cold ashes. Blackberry tendrils probed their way over the charred remains.

Hillary pointed to a thicket of saplings and led the way through the young trees to a clearing. About twenty feet beyond, stood a structure the size of a double-car garage.

They approached the outbuilding. Roger stretched up and peered into the grimy window. "Can't see much. A workbench against the wall." Bright sunlight streamed in from behind him. He turned. "Can you tell what's on that bench?"

She stepped up onto a log and looked in. The glare of a sunbeam spotlighted the legs of the workbench. Getting down, she took a napkin from the picnic hamper and wiped smudges off the window. She refocused her scrutiny. *Was that a saw?*

"Roger."

"Yeah?"

"It's a saw."

"Saw?"

"Yeah, and knives. Looks like they're coated with stuff. Might be dried—"

The noise of a muted thud from inside startled Hillary. She jerked her head toward the road. "Holy Mary," she whispered and jumped down from the log. "Let's get out of here."

They hurried back through the trees and past the ashes to the road.

"Got Ed's phone number in your cell?" She was panting.

He shook his head, so they ran back to her cottage. She grabbed her phone, punched in Ed's number, and told him what they had seen and heard.

* * *

Ed and Walt met them in front of the lot and parked on the opposite side of the road. The detectives followed them in past the ashes and through the saplings, weapons in hand. Hillary's heart thudded, packing her veins with cold blood.

"There." She stopped and pointed straight back. "Off to the left a bit."

Ed squinted as he made out the shape of the building, a dark mass, like a concrete war bunker.

"You two stay put," he whispered. "Better yet, get back out to the road. This could get ugly if someone's in there." They didn't argue but followed a safe distance behind.

Hillary watched the detectives approach the old building. They stepped around to the far side of the structure. Guns drawn, they rounded the corner and disappeared from view. Heart pounding, she ran to catch up.

Suddenly, a car engine revved from inside. Hillary and Roger made it to the corner in time to see a rusty Chevy Impala back out of the building.

"Freeze," yelled Ed. "Hands in the air!"

A young man at the wheel stopped and raised his hands, looking straight at the officers with a blank expression on his face.

"Out. Get out and keep your hands in view."

The man turned off his engine and did as directed. Hillary could hardly believe what she saw. He looked like one of the demonstrators from the memorial party last night, his hair slicked back ultra neat.

Ed patted him down and ordered him to clean out his pockets. He produced a Swiss army knife that Ed turned over to Walt.

"Identification?" Ed barked. The man pulled out a wallet, and handed it over.

Ed read the driver's license out loud. "Jackson Samuel Bludfort." Ed backed up and looked for an address on the garage-like structure. He found a faded number painted onto the corner of the building. "Your license doesn't match this address. What are you doing here?"

"I moved. Rented this place till I can find one better."

"Mind if we look inside, now that it's in plain view?" asked Ed, not waiting for a reply.

Hillary stood still, wishing they'd brought a camera. Backup officers arrived and a uniformed deputy stood near the young man identified as Bludfort, while the detectives moved inside through the big open doorway.

In a far corner some kind of skinned animal hung by its legs from an open rafter. Along the facing wall stood a workbench that held a collection of saws and knives. Hillary recognized some of them, smeared with a reddish muck.

Ed peered at the cutting instruments then looked over at Bludfort.

"I was just gonna butcher my deer, get the meat in the freezer," the young man yelled from the dirt driveway. He thumbed in the direction of a dented chest freezer in the corner of the room opposite the deer carcass. "Take a look. That's all there is to it."

"Why not clean up your tools?" Ed glared at him.

"The water pipes here are so dang old, roots growed through 'em, barely get a trickle. Need to wash the cuts before I freeze 'em. Was on my way out to buy some pipes at PriceCuts, put 'em in and take it off the rent."

With a friendlier tone, Ed continued questioning the young man. "Where'd you move from, son?"

Hillary sensed fresh confidence in Ed's manner. It was exciting to see him this way. It reminded her of her father and how he interviewed his sources for newspaper stories, with confidence and calm vigor.

"Down from Shingle Springs to be near Dolly. Love living in the foothills but love her more. She's with PriceCuts. In fabrics. Made me this shirt." Jackson smiled, revealing tobacco-stained teeth. "Looks same as a Pendleton, don't it?"

"Take him in." Ed nodded to the uniformed officers. "We need to ask you a few questions."

"Am I in trouble? Need to get to that meat 'for too long."

"Let's say it's more comfortable talking at our place. I wouldn't worry about the deer if I were you."

Bludfort was escorted to the back of a deputy's car.

Ed leaned into the car window. "Know anything about that fire?" He thumbed over his shoulder in the direction of the pile of ashes on the other side of the building beyond the saplings. "What happened back there?"

"It was that way when I moved in. Got this place cheap 'cause of that smoke smell. Don't bother me none. I'm over at Dolly's most time. She was brung up in Minnesota and fries up a A1 venison chop. Most gals out here cook 'em to death." He rattled on while Ed stood listening.

Ed bent his head further into the car, and Hillary had to move closer to hear. "You been over at the Brookfield mansion?"

"Saw sinning going on, had to stand up to Satan. Me and my God-fearing brothers had to speak out at that abomination. Heard it was coming in the paper. Had to stand up."

"Sure you didn't know about it from keeping watch over the Brookfield fence?"

"Watch, yes, watch and pray, spirit is willing but the flesh is weak." The young man's eyebrows furrowed as he darted his eyes from one of them to the other.

"What's that mean?" Ed looked at Hillary and gave her a slight nod.

She nearly crumpled with relief. That young man didn't look too scary—if he really was the peeper.

The perimeter of the ashy lot was yellow-taped along with the garage-like structure. Neighbors had gathered in the alley, getting up close to the crime-scene tape. Hillary learned from one of them that the outbuilding had been a walnut packing shed, before Morada's groves were abandoned and replaced over the years with its willy-nilly assortment of houses. Each had a different opinion of who caused the house out in front to burn down and why.

CSI techs began picking through the materials on the scene. They searched through the ashes, as well as the shed, finding nothing more of value than what had initially met Hillary's sharp eyes.

She made a mental note to go to PriceCuts later and look for the young man's fiancée. He'd called her Dolly.

THIRTY

Identification

HILLARY RUSHED back to the office and plunked herself down to write up the new development. Roger looked on over her shoulder. She had to keep the details sketchy—as Ed asked— to prevent some facts from getting into public knowledge.

She tried to ignore Roger's presence and submerge her anxiety about being watched. She still carried the self-consciousness that began when her mother started watching her whenever she read her father's stories in the *L.A. Chronicle,* as if gauging the strength of their relationship. Soon after that, Mother had moved out, the summer Hillary turned ten. Not just out, but run off to some Pacific Island with her artist lover. As years passed, Hillary tried hard to suppress feeling neurotic when her work as a reporter was under scrutiny. It was just part of the job—editors and readers, too, always checking for what was right and what was wrong. *Thank God this case doesn't involve any mothers.*

Having witnessed the displays of two grisly dismemberments, little fazed her now about getting these stories whipped out. Early on, she'd been thrilled to have them picked up by papers like the *S.F. Times.* Still, it upped the chances of Charles getting jealous over her byline's big play, and his making public her shameful secret. That could ruin her reputation even though ordinary people might not think it was a big deal to borrow someone else's words. Roger might have to let her go, and the school surely would not want a plagiarist—no matter of how little—teaching the budding journalists.

The *Columbia Daily Spectator* had carried the story after the second body was found. Her gut was in a knot as she'd read Charles' opinion piece and his quoting her firsthand story witnessing the leavings from the two kills. *He must know this is me. Why no word from him?*

He'd had plenty of words for her when they first met. It was just over a year ago but felt like ancient history. He was the senior editor, she one of the incoming journalists at Columbia to get a master's degree. She'd been in deep thought at her computer, propped with her elbow on the desk, chin resting on her fist, frowning over her first story for the student *Daily Spectator.* Charles walked by and tucked a folded sheet of paper under her elbow. Startled, she sat back and read the note. "Love to get to know you better. Dinner tonight?" She looked up. He was staring at her across the room with a sultry smile on his face. Her heart pounding, she nodded. He took her to Sardi's in the theater district.

She loved the dark red walls hung with signed photos of celebrities from all over the world. He laid out his hopes to get hired at the *L. A. Chronicle* as a Hollywood film reviewer. She offered her father's connections. Charles outright admitted he was envious of her contacts, but he was romantic as hell from then on. Until rumors of her father being forced into retirement made their way through the press community. Then, Charles dropped her, cold.

* * *

She snapped her mind back to the present, worried she might someday have to put out a public mea culpa, unlike Jacki Jones who'd never admitted her white-collar crime. She felt sure that Charles would contact her if he wanted to threaten to go public. If only to be mean, true to his conniving nature, expose her out of spite. He must still be occupied with his new hottie out on the east coast, not feeling the urge to rip up Hillary. She reached over to get chocolate-coated biscotti out of the glass jar on her desk. After eating half the cookie, she felt steadied and bent to the keyboard. As she raised her fingers to the keys, a powerful a sense of herself as an organist in a cathedral, about to perform a piece she knew well, flooded her body.

"The young man in custody is an ardent deer hunter who does his own venison processing, certainly skilled enough to mutilate bodies"—and so on, she typed with fervor. She looked up at Roger, who gave a nod and returned to his own desk. She uploaded the story to their website within minutes. She loved the Internet that let a little weekly paper become an on-the-spot breaking news outlet.

Just as she finished, Ed called and asked if she could get over to his office. He wouldn't say why but that it was important.

She stopped for a chai latte at Joe's, a block from the sheriff's outpost, to tide her over. She liked to think her business helped keep Joe from going belly up. Today, she was one of three customers in the shop. She wondered how long he'd be able to keep the little shop going. *Got to run more stories on local businesses.*

* * *

"What's up?" She took the lid off her latte to let it cool and leaned back against the green mock-leather chair in Ed's cubicle. "This is about the size of a prison cell and you have to spend your time in it," she joked. "Who's the good guys and who's the bad?"

Ed frowned. "We're working to put Sam at the scene of both killings."

"Sam?" She blew on her latte and sucked the foam off the top.

"Jackson told us his nickname is Red Sam." He gave her a piercing stare. "How about that name." He bit on his bottom lip. "I know you saw him over in Morada, but Walt wants you to take a look at a lineup."

"Okay." Her shoulders sagged at the thought of this responsibility.

"Let's go." He led her down a short hallway to a viewing section.

Walt was waiting. He punched a button on the wall and spoke into it. "Bring them in."

Five men paraded onto a brightly lit stage beyond the one-way mirror, moving across from right to left. Each had a card in his left hand with a number on it, the first with number one, next two, and so on. At commands from Walt's disembodied voice, the men first faced their unseen gallery, then turned side view, then faced away. They all wore baseball caps.

Hillary gasped. From the rear view, the fourth one in looked like the man she stood behind at PriceCuts' back door a few weeks ago.

"That guy, he's the one who went in before me that day," she whispered.

"Which day?" Ed stood behind her.

"That first Monday, the morning of my interview with Brookfield."

"You sure?" Walt blew his nose on a big white handkerchief.

"I'm pretty sure," she said. "I mostly saw him from behind but got a look at his profile that morning. He had that straight nose and thick eyebrows, frowning when the guard questioned him."

Wish I could see his shoes better.

* * *

Ed and Walt ushered her out into the pale green hallway.

"Does he work for PriceCuts?" she asked.

They exchanged hard glances. "It will be public record," Ed said. "We're going to arrest him. Never did work for PriceCuts. Was there that first Monday for an interview with the meat manager, Stoney."

"But . . ." she frowned. "How could he get in and kill and cut up in that short time?"

"Could have doubled back after for a morning interview with Stoney—had fake ID on him. He's part of a team says they do God's work and send perverts, as they call 'em, to their punishment."

"Okay for Brookfield, but what would he have against Stoney?"

"We're working on it." Ed led her down the hallway to the parking lot entrance. "Thanks for your help," he said, gesturing in the direction of her car, dismissing her. She felt confused over his curt behavior. Was this the real Ed—all business on a case?

Back at the office, thoughts of him evaporated when she saw that her story of Red Sam's arrest had made the national news, including her quotes from local residents. They were both terrified and proud to be the center of attention in little old Morada—perfectly mirroring her own mixed feelings.

THIRTY-ONE

A Fiancée

HILLARY HEADED FOR PRICECUTS, searching for Red Sam's fiancée Dolly in the fabric section, not having a clue what she looked like. There was only one clerk there, though, and it was easy to read the Associate's nametag on the dowdy young woman, cutting some black denim. She folded the cloth, marked the price slip, and handed it to a tattooed teenager. "That will make a great biker costume, but you need some black leather to go with it, don't you?"

"Got the leather, Ma'am." The teen clomped down the aisle and into the men's underwear section.

The short plump woman named Dolly replaced the bolt of denim and muttered, "Hope when I have kids there'll be something else than tats and piercings." She turned to Hillary. "How can I help—"

Dolly's cell phone interrupted with a barely audible buzz, and she flipped it open to check caller ID. Surreptitiously, she turned away and answered in a quiet voice.

Aware of the rule against calls for employees except in the break room, Hillary positioned herself to shield Dolly in case any house security were around.

The fabric clerk listened a few seconds with a frown on her face. "I'll be down as soon as I can get away." She slipped the phone into the pocket of her gathered skirt and fled for the break room in the back of the store.

Hillary followed and sat down at a plastic table, pulling a power bar from her pocket and munching at it while Dolly made a phone call. She didn't seem to notice Hillary in the room.

"Pa, Jackson's being questioned over at the sheriff's." Dolly paused a second. "Yeah, it's ridiculous. But in case he needs one, what's the name of the lawyer you and Mom used after the accident?" She grabbed a napkin off the table and wrote on it with care not to tear it. "Do you have the number?"

She folded and unfolded the napkin, then penned out something else on it. "Thanks, Dad. I can't believe they would hold him on this, just because he was cutting up that buck for you."

She got off the phone and paced along the wall by the bulletin board. On the board hung notices offering reward money for the killer from PriceCuts headquarters.

Hillary bit off another chunk of peanut butter bar. She felt awkward. "Those cheap bastards only put up $10,000 for a reward," she blurted. "They can't stand this bad publicity though customers seem to hardly notice."

Dolly stared at the reward posters. "My Red. He's not like that. Just because he's cutting up deer meat . . ."

A pang shot through Hillary's gut. She swallowed the lumpy half-chewed bite. "Red?"

"He got it for Mom and Dad, that's the sad part." Dolly's lips drooped and her eyes filled with tears. "I call him Red. His hair's nearly black now, but when he was a little boy, it was bright red." Her smile lit up her plain face.

"Why'd he get the meat for them?" asked Hillary.

"After the accident, Dad had to have his amputation. He couldn't go hunting no more." She sniffed. "Red got him a buck this season and was dressing it over in that shed in Morada. He didn't want to mess up my parents' place."

Hillary's stomach began rebelling against the power bar's mealy soy base.

"He knew he couldn't move in with me, my parents and him, too, being so religious. He had to get his own place and we're saving for a house, so . . ."

Hillary tossed the wrapper into a wastebasket, the last third of the bar untouched.

"It was cheap rent, behind a pile of ashes—can't figure why that pile isn't getting cleaned up."

Hillary stared at Dolly. "I was there this noon time. We saw . . ." She rolled her lips around in a circle, then folded them in and bit on them.

Dolly pulled a chair out and sat right next to Hillary, touching her on the shoulder. "What. What did you see?"

"Some saws, on a table or a bench, like a counter."

"So?"

"They looked like they had blood on them and . . ." Hillary bit at her bottom lip.

"And?"

"So we called the cops."

"You?" Dolly jumped up and stood staring at her. "You did this to him?"

"We didn't know anything—the shed seemed abandoned, so we looked in." Hillary felt torn between the evidence and this young woman's relationship with Red Sam.

"That used to be a packing shed when Morada was a going orchard, when walnuts came out every fall by the truckload," Dolly said. "That was the storehouse and the tool shed. They kept tractors and everything in there. Usually had a pump house next to the shed for irrigation."

"But, why was your fiancé there?"

"He rented it, cheap, and put in a bed. When he knew he was going to get a buck for Dad—he's a great shot—he got himself an old second-hand freezer for the venison. He's not a killer." She burst into tears. "I've got to get him this lawyer's number. But I can't leave 'til my shift's done. PriceCuts, no excuses or we lose our jobs." She scooted back and stood. "This break's too long already!"

Hillary watched Dolly run out of the room. She began to wonder if Red Sam really was the man she saw that first morning—a couple other guys at PriceCuts looked similar. She phoned Ed. She would have to break the news that her line-up identification was shaky—then maybe he would get even more curt and business-like with her.

Be just as good to find out what he's really like sooner than later

THIRTY-TWO

A Failure

THROUGH THE ONE-WAY MIRROR, Ed and Walt watched Jackson, sitting in the small interview room alone, his hands clasped and resting on the surface of the tan metal table. The young man twiddled his thumbs.

"He's got the skills but what motive?" Walt glanced into the donut box he'd brought into the observation room.

"Simple hatred that he'd been offered such low pay, at a butcher's assistant level? He wants to get married, needs money for a house ..." Brainstorming theories was a part of the job Ed enjoyed.

"Before this, he worked in the foothills at a tiny market, paid less than PriceCuts," countered Walt.

"Anger that Brookfield had invited Dolly to one of those Morada parties?" Not likely but possible, Ed thought.

"How would that explain the meat market manager killing then? That meat guy Stoney was righteous as Job in the Bible." Walt frowned.

"Are we sure?" Ed parried.

"Seems they were the all-American couple. Last year, PriceCuts drove their small market out of business. John Stoney had motive to kill Brookfield, except they're both dead now." Walt studied the selections in the donut box.

"How about Stoney's wife, Sarah? Angry at both the global giant and her weak husband for wrecking their small town security?" Ed shook his head as Walt reached for a glazed apple fritter.

"Nah, she's the soul of sweetness, nearly catatonic over Stoney's death. Plus, she's not strong enough, even if she was skilled." Ignoring Ed's disapproval, Walt bit into the fritter and began chewing, flakes of glaze falling onto his ample shirtfront.

"Who else has PriceCuts put out of business? That Middle Eastern doc. He had his own optical shop over on Main Street until PriceCuts moved in outside the city limits. Took only a month before his business vanished, couldn't match the prices." Hillary had mentioned her impressions of the doctor to Ed after her visit, and they made sense. "Now PriceCuts has let him set up inside there, but you can bet he's not making big money. He's got the halal issues and Hillary says there might be some kind of scandal around his wife's pregnancy."

Ed stood up and stretched. "We could take another look at Zasimo since we're having trouble putting a lock on Jackson."

At that moment, Hillary phoned to tell Ed about her talk with Dolly and need to rescind her identification, which was just as well. Jackson may have been the peeper but there was no solid evidence even on that score. They put Jackson through a final interview and came up with nothing except his being in line that Monday morning with the ashes on his shoes and demonstrating at the memorial party—it wasn't enough to hold him.

Ed felt a touch relieved to let the young man go, but they were still so far from success on this case. No lab results yet on DNA scrapped from inside the salt and pepper wig. Nothing on Hillary's suspected body parts finds, either. He might have to light up a corona before too long—the tension was maddening.

Failure. Again.

THIRTY-THREE

Melvin, the Good Neighbor

I HUMMED GETTING READY for Sarah's visit, a glass of Zinfandel close at hand. She needed help with John's funeral arrangements. She didn't have any family in town and her kids couldn't get off from their east coast jobs for a few more days.

After slicing a lamb loin into inch-and-a-half thick chops, I fingered the silky texture, nearly the same color as the Zin, expecting Sarah to show up at the back door any minute.

The sound of a knock followed by the click of a latch announced she'd come to the front instead. I rushed to the entry and caught her as she fell into my arms, trembling.

"Barely made it up the front stairs . . . couldn't get 'round to the back . . . sorry." She was short of breath from the walk just three houses away.

Sarah'd moved in as a young bride back when I was about ten, on this block in the old section of north Lodi. Moved in with John, and they worked alongside my father in Stoney's Market. Most of the neighbors were in groceries, meat or produce like us.

"I know, I know." I held her, this woman who seemed old enough to be my mother, held her and smoothed her white hair, half fallen out of the braid she had taken to wearing in the last few years.

"I don't know how I can make it without him," she whispered, sagging against my chest and laying her cheek on my shoulder.

I never realized she smelled so good. Her cinnamon scent took me back to when Mother used to bake streusel kuchen. I stood in the small dark entry, transfixed with a gentle pleasure. After Mother died, I'd been lonely in the evenings, but then John closed the market and all I could feel was hot rage—rage at him and Sarah both for being gutless. Could have tried harder. But holding her like this, I wondered if it was fair to blame her for the business failing. Wasn't it more John's responsibility?

"He was a great guy, the best," I said, knowing I couldn't let on how I really felt. Much less what I'd done about it to try to wake people up to the evil superstore. "Come on in. I'm fixing your favorite, lamb."

"I don't think I can eat anything. Really, I feel sick." Sarah left my side and padded into the kitchen. "Even Pepcid AC doesn't help." She sat down and sighed. "Nothing seems worth getting out of bed anymore, now that he's gone—and in such a . . . . What kind of a monster could . . . ?" Tears spilled down her cheeks, and she wiped at them with the edge of her long-sleeved jacket.

"Must have been a medical person, don't you think?" I poured her a glass of Zinfandel. "The cutting was so neat. I heard." When she winced at my frankness, I took a different tack. "Don't think about it, Sarah. The police will get him. Have faith." I turned to the lamb chops. "I do."

She pushed away the red wine. "Have you got any 7-up?"

I poured her a glass of the clear soda and got out some saltines and cheese. "Maybe we should save the lamb for another night?"

She nodded and sipped in silence as I puttered around the kitchen, putting away the red meat and slicing up cold chicken breast for myself. Next time I looked, she was leaning against the breakfast nook wall, and I realized she could barely sit up straight.

"Let's try it again tomorrow," I said. "It's my day off, and I'll get the priest to come, too. Finish your snack, and I'll take you home for some shut eye." I went to my room, shook out a couple sleeping pills, and took them to her. "Have one of these in an hour if you can't fall asleep."

She looked at me in kind of a stupor, wrapped the pills in a napkin, and pocketed them. I helped her down the stairs and along the sidewalk to her front porch. "I'll be over about four tomorrow afternoon." She looked wan and frail as she closed her door. *She doesn't understand how she helped bring this on herself. Sad.*

I took a quick jog up and back down the street, like I used to for public relations' sake, and stopped to chat with a couple neighbors. These were folks whose charities I'd helped support with my premium sausage for pancake breakfasts, ground round for spaghetti feeds, chicken chunks for barbecue kabobs at the school carnivals. These were people who'd been loyal customers at Stoney's over the years. But I could see them changing right before my eyes and I couldn't seem to put a stop to it.

At the curb, old half-blind Mr. Albrecht was struggling to get a new TV out of his trunk. "Can I give you a hand?" I asked my neighbor.

"Sure can, sonny!" He turned to look at me, his lower eyelids drooping.

As I hefted the carton up and out, I could see the PriceCuts tag on it. "Too bad they don't have delivery service, the way we used to deliver from Stoney's, eh?"

"New times, got to keep up with 'em," he said. "Developer's been around trying to get us all to sell. Heavenly Acres, he's calling it. Too close for comfort, ask me. Haven't you seen him?"

"Damn greedy guts. House twin to mine next door already sold and the Baders moved out. People will catch on one of these days." I toted the TV into his house and got it going for him.

We watched the start of "America's Most Wanted," but at the break, a commercial for PriceCuts came on, and I began to feel feverish. "Got to get home," I said.

Rain had started in, cooling me down, and I kept on walking as dusk crept over the sky. I passed by my place and on down to visit Father and Mother in the cemetery at the end of the road, closed now to through traffic. I brushed off the oak leaves scattered on their headstones. They'd spin in their graves if they knew John and Sarah had let Stoney's die. What would Mother start humming as a lament? I knew they would want me to help out Sarah in this rough time, but I felt damn divided over it.

At home, I walked around to the back yard and double-checked the outside door to the basement as I always did, then went upstairs and phoned Father Greg, our parish priest.

"Can you be at my house tomorrow at three-thirty? I can catch you up and we can walk down to Sarah's place together." I rolled the coiled white plastic phone cord back and forth between my thumb and fingers.

After hanging up, I lifted the receiver and let it spin in circles, unwinding the kinks in the cord. Then I placed it back in its cradle.

Getting out the cold sliced chicken, I took my plate out to the living room to catch the next episode of "America's Most Wanted." I sat taking in the details of the unsolved cases, chewing as I watched, trying to pick up tips on not getting caught, so as to keep up the chances people would get my message that PriceCuts kills.

So far, I'd been blessed to get days off at irregular times and escape getting interviewed by those clueless sheriffs. I prayed Mother would keep up her heavenly intercession.

* * *

Next day I puttered around in the basement on my day off, sharpening my knives and tidying up the shelves, proud of the parts in the glass jars that I could use later to underscore my lessons. They were keeping well.

At three-thirty the doorbell rang, and I went up to find the solemn young priest, precisely on time. It was soothing to know there were some things that didn't change.

"Come on in, Father Greg. Sarah's falling apart and she needs our help."

"How long were they married?" The priest followed me back to the kitchen.

"When I was around ten, so that was . . ." I reached into the fridge and took out the lamb chops I'd rewrapped last night in white butcher paper, left over from closing the meat market in Stoney's. "They must have been married in the 70s. Yeah,

191

they marked their thirtieth a few years ago in a double celebration for John's parents' golden anniversary, too. Now he and Sarah will never make theirs. Damn PriceCuts."

"What does PriceCuts have to do with it?" Father Greg held out his hands to take the basket of bread and bottle of wine I offered.

"John was never the same after that outfit opened last year and our business went downhill. He'd never have been working at PriceCuts if they hadn't killed his business." I didn't mention the greedy multinational had also killed my little meat market inside Stoney's. Talking about that'd make me so outraged I couldn't be around any priest. "Let's go."

When we reached Sarah's clapboard bungalow, we stopped. All the shades were pulled down.

"Jeez. Come on, this is going to be tricky," I said, leading the way around to the back. I had to knock a half-dozen times before the door opened to reveal her pale face.

She held open the screen door so we could come in and set down the food. Slumping into a kitchen chair, she rubbed her left hand over the speckled gray Formica tabletop.

Tears ran down her cheeks as she looked straight at the priest. "Sorry, Father, I can't help myself. I know he's supposed to be in a better place, but . . ."

"God rest his soul, he is surrounded by angels, and with his parents. They're protecting you from above." He scooted his chair closer to hers and reached out to hold her small hands. "It will be a beautiful service, Sarah."

She stopped crying and gazed red-eyed at him. She started laughing, a high tinkling laugh, verging on hysterical. "His service. Our children are coming."

"Right. Do we want a rosary? How about after the service?"

"The coroner's office says the body won't, won't . . ." She began to sob.

Father Greg patted her on the back from his awkward position seated at the dinette set. "Put the food in the fridge," he mouthed to me.

Sarah reached out, grabbed two napkins and clamped them over her eyes and mouth.

Father Greg sat back. "That's the way," he murmured as Sarah rocked in her chair and rubbed at her face with the white paper napkins.

I put the lamb chops in her fridge and opened the bottle of Zinfandel. Pouring three glasses, I sat at the table and slid a stemmed glass over to the widow and one to the priest.

"Come on, Sarah, have some. It's red, good for your heart," I urged her.

Sighing, she reached out for the wine and twisted the stem of the glass around. "Anyway the coroner said the body . . ." She sipped at the wine, her brown eyes filling with tears. "He would be ready in three days or so. We should plan, yes." She set down her glass and pressed the base flat against the gray Formica with both hands. "John wanted to be buried in St. Mary's cemetery, up in Sacramento, Father. He loved the Dia de los Muertos march up there.

"Our kids thought it was gruesome, but he collected skulls of all kinds—ever since his open heart surgery, John loved the Day of the Dead." Her eyes watered up. "Kept bragging he'd cheated Death." She shuddered in a half sob. "I told him nobody cheats death, but he would laugh it off—until PriceCuts came to town.

"Over the last ten years, we've marched in the Day of the Dead parade up at St. Mary's. It would be a comfort to have him laid to rest there and go be with him that way every year, call out his name. Kind of like a party ending up with a mass at that altar all decorated up in front of the big blue Virgin Mary." Now dry-eyed, she looked intently at Father Greg.

The priest nodded, writing in a small black notebook. "So, do we want a rosary? Or?"

"I think just a mass, here in town. Then burial up in Sacramento after. It'll be a sort of late Los Muertos at the graveside. I was able to get him into the veteran's section. A plot for him and one for me." She blew her nose and stood up to gather her clumped napkins and toss them into the bin under the sink. She took in a deep breath and leaned against the kitchen counter. "Where's that food you promised me, Mel? The kids are flying in to Sacramento day after next and getting a van transport here. I need to get back my strength."

Relieved she was returning to normal, I got out the chops and Father Greg lifted the cloth off the basket of French bread.

"Bread, wine, and red meat. I can see you've put together a man's meal." She laughed.

"Nope," I chuckled. "Mother taught me the value of balance. Don't fill up on meat alone." I set out a bowl of carrot and celery sticks tossed with black olives and sweet red peppers. "Dig in. Call these our appetizers." I placed the clear glass bowl on the table and got out three dinner plates from Sarah's cupboard. I'd eaten in this kitchen for years and knew where everything was kept. Pulling out a thin carbon steel knife, I tested the blade by dragging my thumb perpendicular over the edge— good and sharp, the way I liked them.

"Melvin has been so helpful, beyond neighborly," Sarah said, touching Father Greg on the shoulder and nodding at me. "I'm starving now!"

I cut into the burgundy-red chops. "They'll cook faster if I slice them thin." I turned the gas fire on high under her frying pan. "Can't beat this cast iron! I love it that you and John stuck by the tried and true. For the most part, anyway."

"Wish we could have held out against PriceCuts," Sarah said, looking glum. "That's when all our troubles started."

"You said a mouthful, neighbor." I drizzled grapeseed oil onto the smoking hot skillet.

THIRTY-FOUR

A Burial

AFTER A DREAMLESS SLEEP, Hillary woke to a gray dawn the morning of John Stoney's funeral. The damp air and earthy smell of Morada invaded her senses as she took a quick jog along the misty roads. Breathing in deeply to get herself energized for the service, she felt like a ghoul, eager to attend the somber event to get another sizzling story, maybe another exclusive since Sarah had not made the burial arrangements public.

Almost halfway between All Souls' Day and Thanksgiving, it could just as well have been sunny in the extension of hot weather they knew as Indian summer. But a dark sky swollen with rain loomed as far as the eye could see. Hillary knew if it poured up in Sacramento at St. Mary's Cemetery, there would be little chance of a Day of the Dead procession from hearse to graveside, like Sarah had said she wanted after the mass.

Roger drove the two of them to the funeral in his Mustang. They approached the parish church, stepping on sycamore leaves layered along the sidewalk. Hillary picked up the smallest perfect leaf she could find and tucked it into her pocket, a habit from childhood. Her father'd made sure she participated in Sacramento's St. Ignatius church community as a child, and she loved the sensuous rituals of the Catholic Church. In particular, she adored the Virgin Mary, a figure that filled the cavity in her soul after her mother ran off to the South Pacific. In the past few years, Hillary had abandoned the virgin, but felt a hunger for her come pouring back as she entered the sanctuary.

The church was crammed. There was standing room only for the eleven o'clock service. She assumed many mourners were John's customers from the past, plus some she recognized from PriceCuts. Sarah and what looked like her son and daughter stood stiff and straight near John Stoney's simple casket. It was closed, of course. Hillary tried to block out the images burned into her brain that morning she and Jacki discovered his severed parts in the design kitchen in that macabre showcase display. *Holy Mary, Mother of God, in your mercy knit him together.* She prayed the cops hadn't needed Sarah to identify his mutilated body.

Up in front, the daughter fingered a spray of orange marigolds on the casket and bent to touch her forehead to the wooden lid. Then she knelt down and adjusted a couple of framed photos sitting on graduated easels atop the forest green carpet supporting the casket containing the remains of her father.

She turned to her mother and brother, and nodded to signal their move into the front right pew. Flanked by her grown children, Sarah dropped onto the kneeler.

Hillary and Roger moved up toward the front. A huge dried arrangement in the shape of a cornucopia stood on a tall easel. Hillary peered at the horn of plenty spilling out harvest abundance, wishing she had binoculars to check for parts. No one would do that at a funeral, surely. She felt grateful two Mondays had passed with no new killings.

Near the end of mass, raindrops began tapping against the stained glass windows as if Nature herself was eager to soften the ground and claim what was left of John Stoney's poor body. His son stood at the lectern, introduced himself as Chris, and invited everyone to the graveside burial in a late Dia de los Muertos service in honor of his father. He said it would be up at St. Mary's Cemetery, where his grandparents were buried. Hillary noticed he offered no invitation to a gathering afterward. What a contrast to Steven's loud and public memorial.

Roger and Hillary joined the procession of vehicles trailing the hearse and family limousine up to Sacramento. The rain fell heavier as they drove north. By the time they reached St. Mary's gates, it was pouring and there were just a half dozen cars still following the hearse. At the graveside rite, the young priest, hurried along by the downpour, gestured over John's casket, mouthed a few words, and then turned to escort Sarah back to the limo. There were a handful of people left by this time, the rain having become a torrent.

Hillary pulled down the hood of her jacket, but not enough to obscure a view of the Stoney's grown children. The son lifted the lid of his father's casket an inch or so to make room for his sister to push something inside, then he let the lid fall closed. Hillary wondered what they put in—thinking of the tiny Jack Daniels bottles she'd tucked into her own father's casket.

The brother and sister nodded to the cemetery employee standing nearby. Hillary watched them back away toward the limo where their mother was waiting. *A family man, unlike Steven Brookfield. What kind of person would kill two men so unlike each other?*

A man stood near the casket, gazing at floral arrangements piled up on the bright green Astroturf laid over an earth mound built from excavated dirt. Stoney would be lowered down into the hole as soon as they left. Hillary noticed a bulldozer a discreet distance away, ready to bite into the dirt like a mechanical vulture and regurgitate it over the top of the casket.

The man near the casket looked familiar when he looked up past them into a far distance. Then his glance shifted, and he waved in Hillary's direction across the marigold-heaped casket. He walked over.

"A sad day." He peered at them with eyes squinted to keep the rain out. "Aren't you the local reporter lady? I'm Melvin."

Hillary nodded. "Horrible," she agreed, grateful the rain boots she'd found at PriceCuts last week were keeping her feet on the dry side. She folded her raincoat hood back, the better to see him. Wasn't he the man in the store that she'd followed back to that meat cutting place? She felt a bit more edgy.

"I'm going over to the house," he announced.

"You were close?" She felt inane saying the obvious.

"Neighbors, worked together. Hell of a way to go. He loved this Day of the Dead stuff, though, thought he cheated death." Melvin looked at Roger.

"You know Roger Ingram?" Hillary gestured toward her boss and buddy. "Runs *The Acorn*, the old *Clarion News*."

Melvin nodded, then shook his head like a dog getting out of a river, raindrops flying off his slicked-back, short dark hair. The three of them watched as the family disappeared into the limo. A man in a black suit put several flower arrangements into the front seat and slammed the door shut. Roger and Hillary stomped their feet on the wet grass.

She turned to Melvin. "So, where is their house?" It didn't seem right barging in at a time like this, but Hillary felt guilty she hadn't helped Sarah when she'd reached out in the coffee shop. Hillary wondered at this growing attachment to Sarah. *My own mother's never even phoned in twenty years, could be dead as far as I know. But, what do I care?*

"Follow me." Melvin pointed to an old red Dodge Avenger. "I'll keep a lookout for you in the rearview."

Hillary got into Roger's Mustang and they tailed Melvin, having a hard time keeping the red car in sight as he sped down I-99, south from Sacramento back to Clearwater.

"An odd guy, that one," said Roger. "Weird vibes."

"I've seen him over at PriceCuts. He's different but seems okay." He was the man she'd followed into that freezing backstore. Hadn't Ed interviewed all the employees? Hillary combed her fingers through her damp hair. She wanted to be with Sarah's family, see how it was going. Maybe even weave this tragedy into a feature later on?

"Too bad about the ceremony getting rained out." Roger sped south. "All those orange marigolds and crepe paper streamers, just drenched."

"I never paid much attention to Day of the Dead, myself."

"Mom and Grandpa used to take me to the los Muertos procession each year, drive up to St. Mary's Cemetery and march holding wooden crosses decorated with Grammy's picture. We wore skeleton masks. It was fun." He looked at Hillary with a smile. "Some people get hooked on it."

She wrinkled her nose. Sounded morbid to the max, and John Stoney's obsession with it almost a forerunner to his tragedy.

THIRTY-FIVE

A Mother

SARAH, FLANKED by her two children, sat on her living room sofa opposite a fireplace decorated like an altar. Her daughter was staring at Hillary. There was no fire in the fireplace even though it was a rainy and cold day. Instead, lacy streamers with cutouts of skulls and flowers hung down from the mantle. Hillary moved near the display, feeling uncomfortable. She studied the mantle crammed with photographs in frames, sugar skulls, candles and orange marigolds. One candle in a tall glass cylinder had the Virgin Mary of Guadeloupe painted on the outside, with the flame dancing behind her, inside.

Hillary figured the photos were taken years ago for the most part, though there was one recent one of John Stoney in the style PriceCuts used for ID tags, but blown up larger. She felt entranced by a group photo of what must have been John years ago, surrounded by three laughing women. He was seated on a big round rock and the women stood behind him in a semi-circle, arms entwined.

She felt Roger tap her shoulder, breaking the spell. He nodded in the direction of the grieving family. On an overstuffed chair perpendicular to the sofa sat the young priest who had officiated, eating a piece of red velvet cake and drinking Budweiser out of a can as he spoke to the daughter, sitting near him.

"Millie, I hope you and your brother can be here for Los Muertos next year up at St. Mary's. I'll try getting assigned to the mass." He could eat, drink and talk at the same time as if he'd had formal training at it. Sarah was slumped against the shoulder of her son. Hillary looked around the small space, feeling awkward and out of place in the intimacy of their grief. Melvin walked in from the dining room as if he owned the place.

Hillary edged between the maple coffee table and chintz sofa, leaned forward and put her hand over Sarah's. "I'm sorry for your loss." *They need smaller furniture for such a tight space. What am I thinking! Jacki's marketing must be getting to me.* "A shock for all of us," Hillary murmured, noticing Millie shooting hateful looks her way.

"So hard for you, dear." Sarah frowned as tears glistened. "I can't imagine. Don't want to." She must have heard Hillary was at the scene when John's body was discovered. Millie hugged her mother and glared at Hillary as if she were cutting into her mother, wounding her deeper. *Nice of Sarah to think of how I felt. Wish I'd been able to answer her cry for help at Joe's.*

"I was covering the opening of the Design Center and the excitement of having Jacki Jones in town, so . . ." Hillary felt like she needed to apologize, like the killing might not have happened if she hadn't been there to observe the outcome.

Sarah raised her hands to cling to Hillary's. "You live here in town, honey?"

"Down in Morada, renting a cottage."

Sarah sniffed a couple of times and let out a loud sigh. "Nice little forest, there. Kids want me to move back East." She closed her eyes, humming a faint, low tone in reply, like the tail end of OM in meditation. Hillary noticed that Sarah was still beautiful, her skin smooth as the shell of a mature acorn. Melvin stared at Sarah, from across the room.

"Mom's tired," said Millie, standing. "Let's get you a drink and give her a minute." She grabbed Hillary's hand and pulled her out past the dining room, through the swinging door into the kitchen.

"Listen," she hissed, turning to face Hillary. "My mother doesn't need any nosy reporters coming around now. Can't you see that?"

"I'm not like that," Hillary replied, shocked. "This is—"

"Leave her alone," Millie interrupted.

Paralyzed, Hillary stood wordless. *Does she think I'm going to write something bad about her family?*

Roger entered the kitchen and put an arm around Hillary, steering her back into the living room. They walked past Sarah and her son, now deep in conversation with Father Greg and another priest who had taken Millie's spot on the sofa.

Roger opened the front door to motion Hillary outside. The rain had stopped but water covered the ground. Shallow puddles on the neat front lawn glistened with reflected light from the old-fashioned street lamps, lit early now that Daylight Savings was over. "No need to say goodbye," he advised.

Hillary knew it was time to leave Sarah. For now. She walked out and looked back at the house, taking a mental snapshot. Must be Sarah's blue sedan in the driveway.

They worked for an hour at the office, writing a story on the funeral mass and the soggy and late Day of the Dead burial. Hillary ran out of things to write about. She couldn't shake a premonition that something else was coming down the road. Something worse.

She didn't want to go home alone on this gray evening, and Roger agreed to keep her company. No worries over getting romantically entangled with him.

* * *

Back at the cottage, she hung her flimsy jacket on the rack in the entry and kicked off her still-damp boots. Padding barefoot to her room, she changed into sweats, and then returned to see Roger had a fire started and was talking on his cell phone.

"But are you any closer?" He looked up and wrinkled his nose, pinching his thumb and forefinger to close off his nostrils, as if something smelled bad. She guessed he was talking to Ed by the mixture of tones, alternately pleading and demanding. She went in to pour a glass of wine, thinking how the detective seemed at times almost eager to put up with their involvement in the case. She felt the sexual tension between herself and Ed and wasn't sure where to go with it.

God, what a long day.

Roger ended the phone conversation and turned his attention to Hillary. "That Ed, he might mean well, but . . ." Roger frowned. "He's not the sharpest hook on the line."

"This is no TV crime drama," Hillary countered. "The bad guy's not going to be caught inside an hour."

"I had to explain to him why I'm so interested." Roger rolled his shoulders in circles, backward and then forward. "At first he thought I was kidding—guess I'm coming across pretty straight lately?" He stood and picked up a thick iron poker, repositioning the firewood to let in more air and knocking a log off the grate. "Damn! Weird how that Melvin from PriceCuts is Sarah's neighbor." He grabbed the fireplace tongs and wrestled the log back into place, sending sparks flying.

Hillary carried her Chardonnay over to the fireplace and sat cross-legged on a cowhide rug in front of the fire. She looked up at him. "Kind of creepy how Sarah's street's a dead-end leading to an old cemetery. Her kids are no help, so far away. She needs a friend. Here."

"I don't trust that Melvin—I think I saw him at Belinda's the night of the Halloween bash. A strange guy," he said.

"He seems almost like family to Sarah." Hillary took a swallow of the white wine, set it on the hearth, and lay back on the worn hide, with a floor pillow under her head. "He's a butcher over at PriceCuts. Maybe ask him to get us a special turkey? Maybe have him and Sarah over at the end of the month for T-day?"

"'Special,' what does that mean?"

"You know, organic, maybe? Free range, from somewhere local."

"Let's think about Thanksgiving later," Roger said, getting a wine glass out of the cupboard. "Make sure we're feeling grateful by then."

In his humiliation, justice was denied him.
—*Acts 8:33*

THIRTY-SIX

Rumination

I KNEW IT WAS RISKY last time, sneaking John's body out to the demo kitchen on a meat cart during the night. Worked better leaving Steven in his office—still vacant now. Shows the honchos were paying attention, but not the customers yet. Although the crowds thinned down for a week or so after the second lesson, they came back. Even more curious folks swarmed in, too, damn them.

Yep. My third message should be off site, harm the ruthless retailer but not add business by way of the store being sensational news. Hate that Hillary Broome. Thinks she's so clever shifting focus from small markets being the victims to PriceCuts is a victim—oh, sure! Plus, PriceCuts' security is so tight now, you'd think this was the Middle East.

I liked my solitude at the end of the day. Used to get some in the little backstore at Stoney's. Up until that horrible day.

Set up to the perfect stage by a couple glasses of homemade plum brandy, I closed my eyes to watch my movies. Couldn't help replaying that scene, growing angrier each time I reran it.

* * *

"Myself, I always cut up my hens by hand. Anybody can do it with a band saw." I stood as tall as my muscular five feet, seven and a half inches, would take me and faced him off, even though he owned the place. "Got to sharpen your knife so it'll slice a hair."

Seated at an old card table, John had leaned forward and frowned up at me as if he didn't know me, even though we'd worked together for decades.

I demonstrated, at ease in the back of Stoney's Market amid the ever-present stacked cases of canned and dry goods. "You start by laying her out on her back and slicing the skin in a half circle at the top of the thigh." I flittered my fingers in the air over the table as if it were my meat counter. "Do the other leg next, before you drop your knife and pop out her thigh bones. Snap 'em quick and neat so you can see the round white eyeball end of the bone staring at you."

John scowled, looking older than his years. "Sarah and I appreciate your competence, Mel, but we have no choice, dammit." He slammed his palm flat onto the cardboard table top, making the whole thing shimmy and the office supplies rattle. The pencil cup fell over, top heavy with the weight of the magnifying glass John had added a couple years ago.

I carried on. "Then you finish off slicing, so the thigh and leg drop off as one, no loose skin dangling or bone splinters to clean up. Nope." Deep in my heart I wanted him to appreciate my artistry. Though I would never call it by that name, trained to be stoic by my father, from a long line of butchers.

John shook his head, his face looking contorted, as if in pain. "Look at me, Mel. Sure we had that upswing after the mad cow scare, but PriceCuts came in barely outside the city limits and stole our regulars. The old German meat shops are sucking up money from newcomers moved in from the Bay Area. We're stuck in the middle. Wouldn't do this if we weren't forced to."

"Don't give me that. You know what this place means. It's Sarah's idea, isn't it?" I glared at him and stabbed at the table with the pointy tip of a letter opener.

"It's just business—costing us more to stay open than to call it quits. Sarah and I hate it more than you do."

I fell silent in the cool, dark space at the back of the market, the only place I had ever worked in all my years. Or ever wanted to work. I stared down at the brown asphalt tile where it was chipped in the shape of a fan and remembered how proud of me Mother was.

"Nobody likes it, Mel, I swear . . ." John bent forward and looked up at me with sorrow.

My chest caved in and shoulders sagged. "All right, all right. I give up. What do you want me to do? Buy packaged meat from the Midwest and rewrap it here?"

"Aren't you listening? It's too late. I've been telling you for months, we've got to give up the store." Frowning, he stood and towered over me, rifling his fingers over the ragged ends of his overgrown gray crew cut. "Next week's our last. Take Monday off. Go see Brookfield, the HR guy over at PriceCuts. They need experienced men. They're even putting me on the management track,

209

and at my age. They're not the devils you've got them figured to be."

John pushed open the saloon-style doors leading out into his little store, leaving them to flap back and forth a few seconds before they came to rest in a closed position. In the dim backstore, I fiddled with stuff on the table, picking up the magnifying glass and waving it over a stack of pale green advertising flyers Sarah had made up, promoting local free-range chickens at half the usual price per pound. We used to print tiny twenty-dollar bills as the flyers' border and remind folks how far their money went with us. The images made shopping here seem fun, like playing with Monopoly money.

Did she know these would be the last ads before the greedy bastards squeezed us out of business? She was a quitter, that Sarah. Sitting at the flimsy folding table that served as our desk and our fathers' before us, I felt myself beginning to crack into pieces. My hands opened and clenched, as I rubbed them over my thighs, rocking but finding no comfort.

* * *

Same back then on that hellish day as today. There was no justice. I couldn't cave in without trying to slay the giant. Sarah would be the perfect one to help get across the message. She should feel honored my letting her be part of the lesson this time, make up for her cowardice.

THIRTY-SEVEN

Recognition

JACKI JONES PHONED the next afternoon, all excited, and offered Hillary an exclusive update on the progress of reconstructing the Design Center for the rescheduled opening. It amazed Hillary that PriceCuts was still going through with it, after two gruesome murders. Didn't look like they would let anything stand in their way.

She had to work over at the college helping students put the paper to bed but agreed to run next door to the store afterwards. The celebrity designer was such a hot news topic that whenever she said "jump," Hillary found herself feeling like a trained dog, eager to obey. Jacki said she'd leave her a pass so she could get into the executive conference room for the update.

* * *

"This room still gives me the creeps," Hillary said, putting her tote down on a side table in the conference room.

"Got to get over it, girl." Jacki flipped through a collection of sketches for the new layout of the retail floor. "No kitchen at all this time," she said.

Hillary looked around the stark white room, recalling how on that first Monday she'd been so horrified and confused. Walking over to the control panel, she brushed her hand lightly over the surface, and sure enough, the wall slid to the right, leaving a gaping opening into the now-empty office that had belonged to Steven Brookfield. It was a relief to see it vacant. Even the carpet had been removed down to the bare concrete floor. "Looks like no one wants to sit in that office ever again." Hillary turned to Jacki, expecting agreement.

"Forget it. That was then, this is now." Jacki raised her head, tossing her new hairstyle, colored like honey drizzled on baklava. "Come on over so I can show you how the customer traffic will flow. Get them to buy more." She grinned her bright and proud smile. "We aren't going to have opaque drop cloths covering it up either, sweetie face, so no surprise to hit you with this time."

"Good thing you've got the new opening on a Tuesday, get past those morbid Mondays." Hillary laughed. She turned back to the panel to close the cavernous space, glancing down at the bare concrete. Where the wall had slid into its pocket, lay a scrap of pale green paper. She bent to pick it up and, not seeing any trash bin, slipped it into the pocket of her blazer. "Ok, lady, show me how you're going to make the public forget what your Design Center opened to showcase last time." Jacki was stimulating to work with, had so much flair that Hillary caught a second wind. A couple hours of absorbing the designer's ideas and plans flew by like magic.

* * *

Dead tired from the long day, Hillary had trouble sleeping, and dreamed of the fireplace mantel in Sarah's living room, of the pictures set out among orange marigolds. One black and white photo showed John and Sarah as young parents with toddlers Millie and Chris, all four holding hands like paper cutouts, their names inked in neatly in the lower right corner. In her dream, Sarah's arms let go of her children—she swam up out of the frame and morphed into a frozen carcass, hooked on an assembly line feeding into a chipper machine. Hillary shrieked as Sarah was dragged into the chipper's maw and spewed out and up in a fountain of acorn-sized nuggets soaring high to merge into a canopy of black clouds.

Struggling out of the dream, Hillary woke up clammy, feeling sick and nervous, to find it was only midnight. It was pouring rain, and she sat at the front room window next to cold fireplace ashes, confused and afraid. She dozed off and on, disturbed by more dreams.

The green scrap she'd picked up in the conference room took the shape of a triangle kite and soared into the sky on a razor sharp line, spinning upwards then plummeting in a dive to earth. Over and over came its silent dance on the stage of a dark sky, lightening bolts sparking off the silvery line and thunder blasting the little kite nearly out of sight. She woke reaching for the kite as it flew into the cottage and skittered side-to-side, worried sick that she'd cut her hand on the sharp line.

She was shocked to find it was eight in the morning. She must have gotten some sleep after all. A shadow of the dream hovered in the back of her groggy mind.

After a shower and a cup of hot French Roast, it hit her. She rushed to the coat stand in the entry, reached into her blazer pocket, and pulled out the scrap of green paper.

Laying it on the table, she studied its raggedy knife shape. A triangle about two inches by four, it tapered down to a point, with printing on it. What was it?

Her blood began to tingle up and down the inside of her arms. She called Ed on his personal line. "You've got to get over to my place, pronto."

"What's up?"

"Come and see for yourself."

* * *

She let him in and pointed to the table. He bent over the scrap and let out a low whistle. Not only were there words printed on it, but below them was a scrawled signature that looked like some wavy hair on top of two eyes and a smiley mouth. There were tears drawn on the cheeks in grease pencil.

"Where's this from?" He spoke in an edgy voice.

The story of what happened last night tumbled out in a rush. "I found it in the sliding wall, the one between the conference room and Brookfield's desk. I think maybe it got pulled back into the slot when I opened the door that first morning, you know, when I was stuck in the conference room and couldn't find my way back to the receptionist's desk."

"Slow down," he said, writing fast.

"I was at PriceCuts last night to cover the story of Jacki Jones' remodeled spaces, opening soon, and I couldn't resist hitting that wall panel again." She gestured to show what she'd done. "This scrap was wedged in the wall pocket. Think the killer meant this as a message?" She frowned at him. "Isn't this something you haven't seen before?"

She read the words out loud. "—toney's boasts Melvin's best sausages—your first link is free." Ed sat silent at the table.

She sat down. "How could your guys have missed it?"

"Did you touch it?"

"Oh God," she said. "I didn't think."

He had snapped on vinyl gloves and opened a clear plastic evidence bag that he turned inside out and used to pick up the green scrap and enclose it. "We'll run it right away."

"Do you think it points to Melvin, the butcher?" she asked. "He used to work at Stoney's, didn't he?"

"We'll get on it." Ed looked relieved and eager, almost refreshed. "Thanks, Wonder Woman. You ought to enroll in the Administration of Justice program along with teaching journalism."

Fear nibbled at the corner of her mind. The way Melvin had steered Sarah around the day of her husband's funeral was more than odd. It was controlling, almost manic.

"That Melvin hovers over Sarah in a weird way. I'm going to check on her." She stood and pawed through the stuff Jacki had given her last night, looking for Design Center sales promotions. "I'll take her a coupon for a free in-home consult. Make it seem like a casual visit."

"Before her meat-cutting neighbor comes calling, let's hope." Ed stood, frowning. "You be careful. Got to take this scrap to the office, match it up to the evidence before we can go get him."

They left the cottage, dashing out to their cars as rain began pounding, drenching the ground.

PART III

June Gillam

THIRTY-EIGHT

A Fluke

ED SPED DOWN THE HIGHWAY, the heavy rain giving him the creeps. It reminded him of the wet fall day when that bastard driver hit Mary Beth and left her to die. The beginning of hell, his crushing failure to find her killer. Five years, but seemed like an eternity of shame and blame. Flooded with guilt, he pulled into a liquor store to buy some Coronas. *Funny how the little liquor stores don't go out of business.* He unwrapped the five-pack of small cigars and inhaled for a long minute. Calmed from their spicy fragrance, he stowed them in his left breast pocket and rushed to the office, relieved to find the rookie Laurel Mendoza at her desk.

Ed waved the green scrap nestled in its clear plastic bag in front of her face. "Look familiar? Hillary found it last night, deep in the sliding door slot between Brookfield's office and the conference room at PriceCuts."

She swept stray blond hair off her forehead and tucked it behind both ears. Swiveling ninety degrees, she fingered through an evidence box and pulled out a bag, twin to the one Ed had dropped on her desk. Pushing them up against each other, she formed a bigger picture from the pieces. At the bottom, read "The old-fashioned pride of Clearwater. S" which fit up snugly to the scrap he'd brought in: "—toney's boasts Melvin's best sausages—your first link is free."

"Exact fit." She traced her finger over the ad's letters. "What do you make of it?"

"Got to be that little butcher from PriceCuts that Hillary's worried about. His name's Melvin." Ed stood frowning down at Mendoza.

"What are you waiting—"

"ALL HANDS TO TYLER ISLAND!" a voice blasted over the loudspeakers. "Levee Break Alert. All hands to Tyler Island Stations. Priority One. This is not a drill." The message repeated four times, causing a tornado of activity.

Mendoza jumped up, pulling on her navy blue uniform jacket, her deputy sheriff's badge so new it hadn't softened the folds of the garment around it yet. "Let's go."

Ed couldn't believe the timing. He phoned Hillary's cell but got no answer. He left a message explaining their emergency flood situation and warning her not to go alone to Sarah's.

THIRTY-NINE

A Free Home Demonstration

"COME ON IN, NEIGHBOR." Sarah smiled at me, displaying her even white teeth as she held open the screen door, then shut the bottom half of the Dutch door after I walked in. "Isn't this rain great! I leave the top part of this door open for the fresh air. I felt full of energy this morning, first time since . . . . You know."

She adjusted her red and white-checkered apron and gestured toward a chrome breakfast table chair. "Make yourself at home. Took out a fryer from the freezer last night, going to cut it up now. Craving the taste and wanted to pay you back for all you've done." She whisked out the chicken from the fridge and turned on the water in her porcelain sink.

I stared at the stream of water flowing over the bird. My muscles felt warm and soothed, drowsy. I could almost hear Mother singing to me at morning bath time.

"Rub-a-dub-dub, three men in the tub and who do you think they are? The butcher, the baker, the candlestick maaaaaaaaaker--that's who they are." She would be kneeling beside the tub, her pink tee shirt getting wet with the splashing back and forth between us.

She would raise one fist over the other as she called out the occupations, not stopping with candlestick maker. "And the butcher is at the top," she used to squeal, laughing and grabbing a sponge to squeeze warm soap bubbles down over my short black curls and thin white frame. I could still feel her

221

wrapping me in that fluffy white towel, blotting with care all over my little body.

Then later we would go down to Stoney's Market to watch Father cut meat with his long boning knife. "That's what's in store for you, Melvin." She would ruffle my hair and beam with pride. "You'll be the best butcher in town!"

Grinning at the memory, I gazed across the room at Sarah, holding the chicken tilted under the running water to wash out the insides. I stood up. "Showed John plenty of times, but never showed you how I cut up my birds by hand, Sarah." I moved over next to her at the deep white sink.

Water splashed over her hands. Her slim knife fell near the chrome strainer basket, and I reached down to pick it up. "You start by laying her out on her back and slicing the skin in a half circle at the top of the thigh."

Her gaze locked onto the fryer I had transferred over to her cutting board. Her knife in my hand danced over the chicken. "You can do the other side next if you want, before you drop your knife and pop out her thigh bones," I said. "Snap 'em quick and neat so you can see the clean round end of the bones staring straight back at you. It's keeping it neat that's the trick."

She looked up at the brass wall clock then out at the driveway, coated with standing rainwater. "Mailman due pretty soon, Melvin." She smiled at me. "You know?"

"You can get the mail any old time. Look here, see how I slice that skin clear around, and the leg and thigh drop right off, no loose skin dangling or bone splinters to clean up."

She wasn't watching me but was staring out the kitchen window.

Damn it. She still wasn't paying attention. "Let's go down to my house. I can demonstrate better down in Father's workshop. You'll love it."

She turned her head and looked at me. "Aren't you feeling well, Mel?"

"I'm fine and dandy. Come on with me, sweetheart. Got some lessons to teach."

She elbowed me aside, but I poked the steel blade tip up tight against her throat. "Leave this fryer be. Finish her up later."

Sarah's body went limp against me.

In tandem, the knife tip at her carotid, we stutter-stepped our way past the doors, leaving them ajar. The rain was making it harder than I expected. As we neared the garden gate, she tripped and fell hard, flat on her face.

"Get up. We've got work to do." I knelt next to her motionless form. She must have fainted. Damn.

The knife in my grip began moving, circling, almost on its own. It arced in the air. "You start by laying her out on her back and slicing the skin around in a half circle at the top of the thigh . . ." I could hear myself muttering.

Sarah's doorbell rang out its slow cadence of Winchester chimes. I froze in place over her limp body, watching until I could see the substitute mail carrier slogging along the sidewalk to the next house, going the opposite direction from where I was headed.

"Sarah." I slapped her face. "Wake up. We're going down to my house. Want to show you Father's knives."

FORTY

An Attempt

WITH A SENSE OF DOOM, Hillary had watched Ed drive off in a hurry. Inside her car, she reached toward the ignition. *Where are my keys?*

She shouldered open the car door and ran back to the cottage. Icy raindrops fell on her hair and spread themselves along her scalp. *Shit.* She yanked up her hood and stepped onto the slippery porch. Hoping hard, she waggled the knob back and forth, a half dozen times. *Damn.* The door was locked. She let go a stream of curses.

The rain soaked her jacket. She looked up at the dripping mat of walnut leaves clinging to gray branches. The Morada forest was crying along with her. A blob of water stabbed her between the eyes like the piercing shock she'd felt the morning she saw Steven Brookfield's white arms spread out on his black blotter.

It can't happen to Sarah.

She thought of going ahead and calling but didn't have Sarah's phone number. So she punched in Roger's cell number and got through to beg him to bring the spare key she'd left with him.

"I don't know how it could have happened. Just come over." She kept the cell phone covered by her windbreaker hood. This cottage was poorly designed, not even a porch roof, no shelter from the rain. "Come now, now, now. I'm worried sick about Sarah."

"I'll drive by her place on the way to—" His connection broke.

"Get over here," she shrieked into the dead phone. "I need you to let me in to get my keys." She snapped her cell shut, pinching her ear in the maneuver to keep the phone dry inside her hood, and slipped it down into her already damp pocket. How much moisture could a cell phone take? Why hadn't she bought a waterproof jacket?

She tramped over to the living room window and tugged on the screen. The old wooden frame gave way with ease and she lifted it up and out, leaning it against the cottage siding. Flattening her palms against the glass pane, she gave it a push upwards. *Holy Mary*. It was unlocked. How could that be after all the care she'd taken?

Shoving the window all the way open, she heaved herself up and over the ledge, drenching the café curtains, and landing on the sofa. From across the room, she could see her keys hanging on one of the wall pegs. She slid the window shut and took an extra second to lock it. Without bothering to change to a dry coat, she grabbed her keys and slammed out the front door.

Speeding north on Highway 99, she thought to phone Ed, reaching for the cell in her pocket. No familiar lump there. *Shit*. She patted all her pockets. No phone. She pulled over to the side of the road, unbuckled her seat belt and searched the seats and the car floor for the cell. *Damn*. She must have lost it while crawling through the window. Well, she'd have to go without it. She had to get to Sarah's. *Focus*.

Back on the highway, she sped north to the Lodi exit, peering through narrowed eyelids and panting to the whack of windshield wipers on high-speed. The pounding rain nearly erased sight of the roads.

She prayed she would remember which house on the street was Sarah's.

There it was. Her reporter's eye remembered without doubt Sarah's car in the driveway. Pulling in behind the faded blue sedan, Hillary yanked the hood over her semi-dried hair and gathered the damp windbreaker tight against her chest. Head down, she darted up to the front porch through the relentless rain. At least she had a porch roof to stand under here.

Knocking on the door, she hoped her intuition was wrong, hoped Sarah would swing open the door, welcome her, and brew her a cup of tea. Better yet, pour them a stiff shot of brandy in this storm.

She knocked again. Louder. Harder. No response.

Following the perimeter of the white clapboard siding, she peered through damp eyelashes into Sarah's windows as she moved around the outside walls. Some lights on. Good.

The single-car detached garage at the far end of the driveway was padlocked. To the left, a picket gate stood open with a clear path to the back door. She tiptoed up the two concrete steps. The aluminum screen door was ajar and the top half of a white Dutch door opened into the kitchen. She shivered, too anxious to knock again. What if Sarah was inside, forced into silence? *What can I do?*

She listened hard. Over the sounds of the deluge from the gray sky, she thought she heard water running. She opened the screen door quietly and pushed the Dutch door further open, enough to slip inside.

Water was pouring into the left half of a double porcelain sink, inside which lay a fat chicken, legs splayed open. She dragged her eyes off the bird and shot hard looks into the corners of the kitchen and under the chrome dinette table. Nothing. She grabbed a dishtowel off the cream-colored tile counter and mopped her face and the hem of her dripping windbreaker, clenching her jaw to keep her teeth from chattering.

She recalled the scene here after John Stoney's funeral, where Millie had hissed at her to get out, that Sarah didn't need any reporters to take advantage of her grief. Hillary didn't think she was harmful in Sarah's world. Her daughter was jealous of someone caring about her mother when she was too far away to be of any use.

She tiptoed through the dining room and into the living room, stopping in front of the fireplace where the display of Day of the Dead paraphernalia seemed a grisly reminder of the trouble Sarah could be in. Overcome with helplessness, Hillary felt stuck on the spot, stricken with fear of becoming witness to kill number three, this time the murder of someone she cared about.

Gusts of wind threw armloads of rain against the windows framing the fireplace and snapped her back to her search. Good thing the house was so small. How had they raised two kids here? She moved softly over the avocado-toned carpet and on into the hallway. *Holy Mary. Sarah really needs Jacki Jones' free home makeover. Have to find her first.*

She stopped every few seconds to listen, feeling like a cat burglar. No one in any of the three small bedrooms nor in the bathroom. Where was the widow who must have stood at her own kitchen sink washing a chicken—how long ago? The only unaccounted for doors looked to be closets, which she opened and searched without finding Sarah.

Back in the kitchen, she slumped into one of the dinette chairs, staring at the water running in the corner sink. Okay. She's not here. Must be eight or ten houses on each side of the street, built in the 20s and 30s. Some simple clapboards like the Stoneys', some two-story Victorians, even a tall stuccoed job with arched windows. Where does that little butcher live? Her good neighbor. Ha.

FORTY-ONE

An Offering

ED FELT SICK AT HEART. *Gotta send someone else to help her.* He turned to Matt, the young intern standing nearby, taking it all in. "Catch up with Hillary, can you? She's on her way to Sarah's, frantic the old lady's in danger. I've got to show up at Tyler Island—we've been preparing all year for flood disasters, since the levee repairs are taking so long."

"You have a gun for me?" Matt's dark eyebrows shot up at the edges and down in the middle, giving him a fierce look. "I can't go save her without a weapon."

"Can't give you sheriff's issue." *He and Hillary already had a connection back in the Morada forest.* Ed pulled out his personal pepper spray, wrapped in a black leather case. "Take this. It's from a gun show last year up at Cal Expo."

Matt held up the four-inch leather cylinder, clamped between his index finger and thumb, and examined it. "How you work it?"

"Haven't you covered these in class? You need to get certified on aerosol sprays so you can use 'em in the field." Ed frowned and took it back, demonstrating how to open the safety strap. "FBI agents have to take a shot to the face and eyes in their training. I've seen videos. It's not pretty."

He showed Matt how to swivel the lock to the open position. "Keep it closed and locked until you need it, but practice aiming the spray path out in the parking lot. Point away from people. Keep track of the wind direction."

"It's pouring out in the parking lot." Matt held the pepper spray away from his body. "Sir."

"Find a place to practice. Supposed to feel like your face is drenched in gasoline and lit with a match, so you sure don't want it coming back on you. I have to go." Ed double checked his gun and mace and rushed out, meeting Walt in the hallway. The office emptied of personnel, swarming out to deal with flooding in the Delta. They'd trained for a massive levee break and how to evacuate stranded animals and people. Ed had to do his job, but he yearned to go rescue Hillary instead, create some kind of happy ending for a goddamn change. *Now Matt will be her hero. If there is one.*

The rain increased in ferocity. Ed pulled out a small corona, clenching it in his jaw and sucking the earthy tang of the unlit tip.

FORTY-TWO

A Hunt

PULLING HER DAMP JACKET around her shoulders, Hillary left Sarah's the way she found it—Dutch door half open and screen door ajar. She was unsure where to go next—the wind had come up, turning raindrops into pellets that beat against her face.

Sucking in her breath, she stepped carefully down the driveway to the sidewalk, turned left and walked up to a house nearly identical to the Stoneys'. Ducking under the shelter of the small porch, she knocked on the door and slid her drenched hood back, not sure why she bothered with it. She blew on her icy hands and listened, trying to hear above the storm. What if no one was home here either?

A muffled shuffling sounded near the door, and then the click of deadbolts. She felt her shoulders slump with relief as the door opened about two inches and an eye topped with a bushy white brow peeped out. Couldn't tell if it belonged to a man or woman.

"I'm looking for Sarah, your neighbor." Hillary gestured toward the Stoneys' house.

Not even a blink.

"You know, your next door neighbor lady, recently widowed." Was that a nod? "Have you seen her? Today?"

Slight shake of the two-inch swath of elder face.

"What I need to find out—" Hillary shouted over the force of the storm, trying to penetrate into

231

the mind of the person in front of her "—is, where does Melvin live?"

No response.

"Another neighbor, the butcher man, if you know him," she added.

The door swung open so fast, she was shocked.

"Come on in, dearie," cackled a very thin, old man. He pushed open his screen door with a veiny hand, blotched with dark patches. Although it was dark in the living room, overall the house seemed the same floor plan as Sarah's, with a fireplace to the right, the dining room straight ahead and a door to the kitchen off further on toward the right.

"Thank you, sir." She looked into his cloudy eyes, not sure if they were blue or gray. "I'm Hillary Broome, a friend of Sarah's," she lied, hoping there was still time for it to become the truth.

"Never seen you," he croaked and fell silent, peering at her, his hands trembling. He backed up toward a straight chair near the door and sat down. "Name's Stefan, Stefan Albrecht," he went on. "Can't see much nowadays, probably shouldn't be driving, can barely turn on my new TV and listen." He gave a giggle. "Used to keep track of all my neighbors, was why Millie asked me to look out for strangers when she left home."

"Do you know Melvin? Know where he lives?" Hillary stood dripping onto the worn carpet. "I know it's nearby, on this street."

"Here you go, missy." He plucked a yellowish towel off the sideboard next to his chair and handed it over. "You'll catch your death." He giggled again.

She mopped at her windbreaker sleeves before she noticed the sweetish smell of stale urine. "I'm worried Sarah might be in trouble. I need to ask

Melvin about her. Where does he live?" Keeping the pungent towel away from her face, she laid it over a wooden drying rack that straddled a floor heater vent. "Do you know?"

"Melvin, yup, know him well. Nice boy." He bent forward on the edge of his straight chair. "Knew his father better, you could say." He looked up at her, his watery eyes gazing into her face. "Sad story, that one." He wiped his eyes with the back of his gnarled hands.

"I'd love to hear it but need to get to his house. Now."

"Young folks in such a hurry. All right, theirs is a fancy two-story, down by the cemetery, same side of the street, but down the other direction." He waved a knobby finger to his right.

After a terse "Thanks," Hillary shot out his front door and down the sidewalk. Afraid of slipping, she stepped over puddles dotting the uneven pavement, in the direction of the cemetery. Walking as fast as was safe, she formed a mental picture of Sarah at Melvin's, sitting down to a glass of wine. It could be happening. But why leave her water running? The stress of losing her husband? Getting forgetful?

FORTY-THREE

A Vacancy

HILLARY TRUDGED through the downpour, passed by a couple bungalow style houses, and came to a pair of shingle-covered Victorians, painted gray and standing tall like old wooden twins. She turned in to the first one. Holding her breath, she went up a few weathered steps and peered at the front porch, high above. What time was it getting to be?

The cloud cover of the storm obscured any light dusk might have offered. She squinted, straining to see inside the house. A placard in the window to the right of the front door announced the house was for rent. Must not be Melvin's place. *Better check it out though.* Careful not to slip on the wet wooden steps, she returned to ground level and took a concrete pathway off to the right, alongside the house, heading toward the rear. No light came from the narrow basement windows along the ground.

Suddenly, country music drifted from the last of the single-story bungalows she'd passed by. She stopped to listen. Tammy Wynette's "Stand By Your Man" was holding its own against the pounding of the rain.

Wishing she had a flashlight, Hillary was grateful for some illumination from the Tammy Wynette fan's windows. Sticking to her path, she rounded the back corner of the Victorian. She could see the outlines of wooden stairs leading up to a back porch and plenty of firewood stacked under the stairs. A stark black opening yawned to the left of the woodpile. One footstep at a time, she walked toward the dark rectangle, as if pulled by some force. Standing in nearly an inch of mud, she gazed at the opening. A door hung free at the side. That must be the way into the basement. But no one lived there.

She backed up a few steps and looked across the rear yard toward what she prayed was Melvin's house. A ramshackle wooden fence separated the twin structures. *Damn*. Have to go out front again and take the sidewalk down to Melvin's.

As she retraced her path alongside the tall Victorian, the front door of the music lover's house cracked open and light poured out onto the sidewalk. The ending lines of Patsy Cline's mournful rendition of "Crazy" wove a spell over Hillary. On an impulse, she strode toward the front door.

"Hey," she shouted. "Hello in there. I need help."

FORTY-FOUR

A New Beginning

IT WAS HARD WORK getting Sarah out of her house. But not that different from all those times I shouldered around a side of beef in the meat cooler, back in the good old days. It was less than a year ago when John's somber talk in the back of Stoney's Market announced the collapse of our world.

Sarah's resistance forced me to keep one arm tight around her wiry shoulders. I held the knife tip pressed to her ribs. The downpour was keeping the neighbors indoors, what neighbors were left now that the land was getting bought up. By the time I got her into the basement through the back door, she was bleeding under her right breast. Not good. Got to keep it neat.

With one hand, I grabbed a bungee, shoved her up against the load-bearing post in the center, and cinched her to it, arms tight to her sides, wrapping the cord around her below the bloody spots on her blouse. She didn't make a sound, eyes closed, but not dead weight either.

I sat on the old futon, part of Mother's basement redecorating a long time ago. Still neat, with the pale cream muslin cover streaked with red and black in an Asian design like an I Ching pattern. How to keep the work clean? Dignify my message? Should have planned ahead better on this one. Getting too impulsive.

Sarah opened her eyes. She looked at the concrete wall across from the futon, the wall my old bulletin board was on. I'd covered lots of it with

Sarah's advertising flyers over the years. Her lips fell open as she surveyed the series of ad jingles plus sales prices. The flyers were meant to entertain as much as attract the locals, who shopped at Stoney's Market back then as regular as going to mass. Most flyers gave space at the bottom to Hermann's Meats—House of Fine Cuts, my father had called it. Too bad he never moved out into his own shop, cared more about the work than the business end of it.

Halfway across the corkboard, another other kind of graphic showed up—my signature happy faces scrawled onto neat white butcher paper, testament to time passing and my growing up to share responsibilities like helping with public relations. I felt warm and safe for a few moments, studying the wall with Sarah.

"Mel." She turned toward me, whispering. "You kept these all this time?" Her jaw sagged and tears flowed down her cheeks. "The whole set, even from your father's . . ."

I gazed at my long-time neighbor and former employer. "You and John, you could have fought them greedy guts."

She shook her head slowly, looking like an old woman in a nursing home hallway, grieving the past.

"Turned gutless on me, both of you." I gave a decisive nod her way and ratcheted up my resolve. *This is for the greater good.*

Tighten the bungee until it bursts her organs, stops the heart, let the core fill with blood since she's standing upright. Once the heart stops, her blood pump is gone.

The meat would be spoiled if the blood wasn't drained, but I wasn't planning to have anyone eat the meat anyways. I wasn't any damn cannibal like those perverts in the news. Plenty of time. All the tools I needed stood handy over on my workbench—all here at home after John closed Stoney's doors for the last day, damn him.

Need to wait for the storm to pass before I can take my new handiwork down to PriceCuts. Displaying the message is essential. Wrap up the cuts neat and put them in the meat case, take along John's heart in a plastic bag. Bring Brookfield's head in the gallon pickle jar. Have to set that in the condiments aisle. That way not even the vegetarians could miss my lesson.

PriceCuts murders the mom and pops, cuts them up and feeds them to you all. Don't you get it? I might write up some labels to spell it out for the sheep in the superstore.

FORTY-FIVE

An Angel

COUNTRY MUSIC POURED through the open door. The twangy lyrics of "Wolverton Mountain" hit Hillary as a warning—she was a stranger wandering this street where there could be a man mighty handy with a gun and a knife. Or for sure a knife.

She neared the music lover's porch. Silhouetted by light from behind, a woman's scrawny figure held a drink in one hand and a cigarette in the other. "What the . . . Who are you?"

"I'm looking for Sarah, Sarah Stoney."

"Get in here, girl." The thin woman crushed her smoke under foot and reached out to pull Hillary inside. "Get you a towel. Just a sec." She came back and handed over a beach towel, dotted with nautilus shells on a faded pink background. "Hand me your jacket," she ordered.

"C-c-c-can't." Hillary's teeth were clenched to keep from chattering. "I'm in a hurry."

"Sure you can." The woman reached over and pulled down the zipper of Hillary's sopping red windbreaker. Meeting no resistance, she peeled one side off and then the other. "I'll set this in the dryer a couple minutes. You get that towel going, hear? Stand over near the heater."

Moving in the direction of a metal wall unit, Hillary hung her head and mopped at her soaking wet hair. *Have to get going. Get a flashlight, get down to Melvin's. If that's where he lives. Maybe that old man doesn't even know.*

239

The woman returned and positioned herself in the middle of a tan sofa, creased into cracks with age. She shook a Marlboro out of its red box. "You was looking for someone."

A paralysis of fear came over Hillary. She sat silent on the edge of a black naugahyde recliner set nearer to the wall heater than was good for it. She watched the woman light up her cigarette and take a deep drag, exhaling and talking at the same time. "Jack Daniel's is good company in the rain." The woman bent forward to place her cigarette on a huge glass ashtray that dominated her turquoise and white mosaic tile coffee table. "Here." She poured a couple inches of amber fluid from a square bottle of whiskey into a clear plastic glass and stretched it in Hillary's direction.

Hillary stared at it without moving, then reached out and took it. *What am I doing, trying to get to a killer's house?*

"You said you was in a hurry. Why now, out in this storm?" The woman stretched out her scrawny arms to pick up her cigarette and glass of whiskey, taking a pull at each.

Hillary inhaled the pungent aroma of the Jack Daniel's, a comfort ever since she first inhaled the spicy scent in her father's highball glass. *If he could see me now.* She tossed the whiskey down in two gulps, letting its fire warm her up from the inside.

"Name's Debbie. What's yours?" The woman stared at Hillary from under dark penciled eyebrows.

"Hillary." She stood and set her glass on the coffee table. "I'm looking for Sarah, your neighbor." She pointed in the direction of the Stoneys' house. "You know her?"

"Sure, John's widow woman. Keeps to herself now. Never answers the door no more, front nor back." Debbie reached out and flicked her long ash into the middle of the ashtray. "Went to the funeral, I did. Rained too hard for driving up to Sacramento. Takes a lot of gas. Think Sarah's mad at me?"

"She might be in trouble, down at Melvin's." Hillary gestured in the direction she was headed. "Know him?"

"Naw." She lit another cigarette and exhaled with a loud huff.

"No? He's not even on this street?" Hillary felt sweat trickle down the small of her back.

"Naw, that Mel wouldn't cause no trouble." Debbie smiled. "Barbecued up all those chickens every summer for church. After Hank had to retire from his diabetes, I couldn't afford to shop at Stoney's no more. But his chicken wings was tasty. Yep, they sure was."

The Jack Daniel's heated Hillary into panic. "Can I use your phone?"

The woman nodded at a rotary dial model perched on a small table not ten feet from the front door.

Hillary traced Ed's cell number in circles on the slow old phone and waited four or five seconds before he picked up. A section of the levee had failed and the waters surging through had stranded a family of five on Tyler Island, forcing law enforcement to head that way. He said he'd sent Matt to help her, and he warned against going alone in her search for Sarah.

"Wait. Wait for him, Hil." His tone was dead serious. "Don't go to Melvin's by yourself." His cell phone cut in and out.

Hillary shouted that she would wait at Debbie's, and gave him the address, but she knew she was lying. She hung up the receiver and turned to see Debbie pouring herself a refill from the Jack Daniel's bottle. "Debbie, I need my jacket if it's dry. Or something more waterproof if you have it. And do you have a flashlight?"

She looked out the window at the storm and then at her unexpected angel, who had smoked her way down to the filter on her latest Marlboro.

"Let me go look." Debbie took a swig of whiskey, crushed out her butt in the ashtray, and disappeared from the living room.

Hillary paced, trying to ignore the squishy sounds from her wet Nikes and the warmth from the whiskey Debbie'd poured for her. *Need my wits.*

* * *

Where has she gone? Hillary walked through a doorway into a square kitchen. No Debbie. She moved past an old wooden table and chairs into a spacious service porch, with a fairly new washer and dryer. The back door stood open and through the screen, lights from a detached garage shone brightly. Hillary opened the dryer door and retrieved her windbreaker, hot from its tumble. Slipping it on, she stepped out through icy rain—verging on hail—and taking care not to fall, got to the garage. Debbie was rummaging around in a big wooden drawer underneath a battered workbench.

"Any luck?" Hillary shouted.

"Found one in the house, but dead batteries." Looking up from a crouch, Debbie brandished a long black flashlight, and waved it in circles like a sword. "I knew Hank had a torch—that's what he called 'em—stashed out here somewheres. Try it."

Hillary thumbed the button on the heavy black flashlight, and a strong beam flooded the ceiling. "Thanks. You've been such a help. I've got to go." She turned toward the street then back to the woman she'd begun to consider a friend. "That is Melvin's house, at the end of the street, yes?" She pointed toward the end of the road. "Next door to the cemetery?"

Debbie nodded and stood, reached over for an orange umbrella lying on the workbench, lifted it by its black plastic handle, and thrust it toward Hillary. "You out on a night like this, cover your head, girl. But don't open it inside here. Bad luck."

Leaving the shelter of the garage, Hillary opened the umbrella to discover it was a piece of Giants baseball memorabilia. It felt like a good luck sword with its straight handle and sharp metal tip.

* * *

Switching off the flashlight to save batteries, Hillary wedged the heavy torch under her arm, clutched the umbrella handle, and moved forward on the slippery sidewalk in the direction of the last house on the street, the one that dead-ended at the cemetery. Passing by the front of its vacant twin house again, she mentally reviewed what she'd learned of the layout, feeling sure Melvin's had the same floor plan.

No porch lights shone as she reached his place, but down near the ground, a couple short wide rectangles of light glowed through the rain. She felt sick and nervous.

Can't just show up at the basement door around back. Don't want to get him suspicious. Can I get away with it seeming like a social call?

The rain slowed to a sleety drizzle. Clouds were breaking apart—moonlight painted them into a mottled field resembling dirty snow. Hillary wedged the umbrella deeper under her left arm along with the flashlight, wishing she had one of those photographer jackets with plenty of pockets.

One step at a time, she ascended his front stairs, the creaks a prelude to the nerve-jangling buzz of the old-style doorbell after she located it—with the aid of the torch from Debbie—and jammed her thumb onto it. She waited. Nothing. She kept up a drumming with the doorbell button, to the rhythms of "Wolverton Mountain," bracing herself to come face to face with this man and what he might be doing with his knife.

FORTY-SIX

The Basement

WITHOUT WARNING, porch lights flashed on. There he was, opening the door for her with a frown on his face. "Hillary, isn't it? What are you doing out in this ungodly weather?"

"I'm worried about Sarah. She's not answering her door but her lights are on."

It seemed to take forever before he reached out toward the rickety screen door. "Come in, you're soaked. Have some plum brandy. Make it myself every year in the basement, from Father's old-country slivovitz recipe. Keep it down there for old times' sake. Been having a few nips myself on a cold night like this." Melvin swung the wood-framed screen door open, but Hillary stood in place.

"Have you seen her? She left the water running in her kitchen sink and I'm concerned about her. No one's home at her place." Hillary narrowed her eyes, not sure what she was hoping to achieve. *If he has her, he won't admit it, will he?*

"No. But she's not in her right mind nowadays, you know. Since John ..." He flipped some switches and motioned her into the now brightly lit entry hall, paneled with golden curly maple. "Come have a shot of brandy, warm up and dry off a bit, then I'll go out with you and look for Sarah. Truth to tell, I'm worried about her, as well."

Hillary stepped into the entry. *Worried, sure.*

"Come on back, I keep the brandy in the basement, same as my father used to do." He led her down a paneled hall, bypassing what looked to be a parlor and dining room, until they reached the kitchen in the rear.

"Careful down the stairs. They're steep." He waved her ahead through a doorway into the basement. Hillary's stomach churned. *Got to go with him.*

Terrified, she gripped the flashlight and folded umbrella under her left arm and grabbed the wooden handrail with her free hand, palms slick with rain and sweat. One wood plank at a time, she descended the stairs, heart thrumming. As she stepped into the cellar, she could see the wall ahead of her, covered with pale green flyers.

Here it is. Evidence against him was plastered all over his own walls. A thrill of fear poured through her veins, the second before she turned to spot Sarah, tied to a center post by wraps of bungee cord. The older woman stared straight at Hillary as she took the final step down to the concrete floor. *Hail Mary. Pray for us sinners now and at the hour of our death.*

FORTY-SEVEN

The Helpless

ED OPENED THE PASSENGER DOOR of a patrol car and slid in, telling Walt to drive. Walt threw him a puzzled look and squeezed his girth behind the wheel, readjusting the seat to accommodate his belly while Ed punched in Hillary's cell number. Waiting through each ring seemed to take an hour. He sucked on his unlit cigar. When her voice message started up, an icy panic spread through his gut. "She's in trouble, Walt."

Walt shook his head. "Nothing we can do about it now," he said and drove in the direction of Tyler Island, where they'd been ordered to go help evacuations. A dozen head of cattle had already been swept away in the raging flood.

The helpless sensation Ed battled these last five years welled up full force. He felt weak and craved the reassurance that rescuing Hillary would bring. His cigar drooping from his mouth, he sat staring out the windshield through the beat of the wipers against the rain, while Walt sped down the road, lights flashing, sirens blasting. *You had to send the kid.* Ed forced his thumbs to find the number in his contact list and get through to Matt's cell phone.

Ed wasn't surprised to hear that Matt's old Chevy was stalled on a flooded street. *That kid is wet behind the ears.* Matt had phoned and gotten put on the Triple A emergency list, but they couldn't say how long it would take to get to him.

Ed told Matt he'd get someone to go pick him up, punched the End button and turned, grim-faced, toward his partner. "Who can I send? Matt got stranded on his way to help Hillary."

Walt wrinkled his nose and pulled a tin from his breast pocket, flipped open the lid with one hand, and managed to lift two tiny white disks of peppermint with his thumb into his open mouth. "Want one?"

Ed took two and shoved them in around his unlit cigar.

Walt swallowed, then moved the tin up to his lips and poured in a few more candies, crunching as he talked. "Why can't that side-kick of hers at the paper, what's his name? Why can't he go pick up Matt? The two of them can get over to help Hillary."

Ed found Roger's name in his contacts and made the call. Clamping his cell between his ear and shoulder to free up his hands, he pawed through the glove box looking for matches. Roger picked up after the first ring.

"Hey, Roger, Ed here. Trying to get assistance to Hillary before she gets herself in trouble. We've got our hands full with this flood, so I sent out an intern to help, but he's stranded out on the highway." Ed slammed the glove box shut. No matches. "Needs to be picked up and taken to help her. She's on her way to Melvin the butcher's house, trying to save Sarah."

"Damn. I was afraid of that," Roger said. He got Matt's location and cut the connection.

Guy knows how to get it in gear. Ed clenched his jaws around the cigar, pursed his lips around the fragrant brown cylinder and thought about praying.

FORTY-EIGHT

The Struggle

THE BASEMENT DOOR clicked shut behind Hillary. Rain pelted against the high windows at the top of the basement walls. As she reached the concrete floor, she about-faced to block the butcher's descent.

"Melvin?" she questioned in a low voice.

"It's nothing." He stepped onto the floor, straddling her feet with his own and pressing his compact body into hers, face-to-face and belly-to-belly. She could smell booze on his breath, feel his muscular legs through his pants. "Nothing against you personally. Except for some of those stories you wrote, standing up for the greedy bastards." His eyes blazed.

Heel of the hand blow. Instinctively her self-defense training kicked in. Fingers clenched into a tight fist, heel of the hand forward, she shoved her right hand up toward his chin. He ducked to the left, grabbed her wrist and twisted her arm over her head, wrenching it high and forcing her down to her knees, prostrate in front of him. The searing pain hurt like nothing she'd ever felt before. Her arm felt torn out of the shoulder.

"You shouldn't have come. Nothing against you. I even liked it when you called me the Python in the paper." He narrowed his eyes and grinned. "But you fell into their trap."

"What trap?" Her voice squeaked. *Stay calm. Think.*

249

"It's between me and Sarah now. You don't belong here." He kicked into her midsection, knocking her flat on her back, then stepped hard on her belly, pinning her to the cold floor while he stretched to grab a coil of rope hanging from a hook fastened to the open joists.

As he reached, she kicked up toward his crotch but missed. He grabbed her by the leg and dragged her across the concrete to a chair in the corner, outside the circle of light formed by the bare bulb hanging in the center. At first, she managed to keep the flashlight and umbrella clamped under her arm, then let those gifts from her country-music angel go rolling under the chair as she scuffled with his compact, sinewy frame.

"You're making it hard on both of us." He panted. "Sit up like a good girl, and I'll bring you some of that brandy I promised."

She made her body go limp and forced him to position her as dead weight in the chair made of sticks. Kneeing her in the groin, he pinned her to the rough wood and tied her to the chair with white nylon rope, squinting as he worked.

"Cutting her up is part of my message. I hadn't planned on adding you." He stood panting.

"But she never did anything to you." Hillary tried taking a calm and reasonable tone.

"She made John give in. It's her fault. Got him to get me crawling to them for work." He glared at her, then over at Sarah.

Bound up with bungee cord to a post in the middle of the room, Sarah stood still, except for her head, which lolled to one side, her jaw working against a terry cloth gag. Guttural moans rolled from her throat.

"Let her tell her side of the story, Mel."

"She's done. Said too much already. Talked him into it." He sat down on a futon next to a workbench littered with tools, bent over at his waist, and ran his long fingers through his short, dark hair. He threw back his head and pointed at the wall covered with flyers, the color of green Monopoly money. "Those were her babies. Kept most of the Valley coming to us. No call to roll over and give up to the greedy giants." He stood and contorted his features then crowded in on his petite neighbor tied to the post, until they were nose to nose. "No call. No call." He was screaming.

Sarah stood immobile, like a statue.

Hillary bent her knee to wriggle her foot around under the chair, feeling for the flashlight and umbrella.

Breaking his connection with the widow, he spun to face Hillary. Enraged, he didn't seem to notice what she'd been doing. "It'll be better if . . ." He grabbed a bottle off a shelf next to the workbench. "If you don't watch. A couple swallows, and you're in another world if you're not used to it." He pulled off a cork. "Got to pour it into a glass. Father would never permit Mother and me to drink from the bottle." He poured an inch of fluid into a heavy glass and held it to her lips.

Hillary jerked her head away.

"You'll like it. Stormy night, warm you up. It was winter that first time I got to taste it, and down here, with Mother." He slipped the glass to the far side of her mouth and grabbed a knife off the workbench to pry her jaw open with the blunt back edge of the blade. He sloshed the brandy into her mouth, tipping up the glass, and shoving it against her clenched teeth. Grabbing her long hair, he pulled her head back, forcing her mouth open, and emptied the glassful into her mouth.

She choked, sputtering and swallowing, spitting half of it onto the floor, and kicked out at him wildly.

"Good, huh? It's slivovitz, from plums. Father made it when he was a boy, in the mountains back in the old country." He stood to the side where her feet couldn't reach him. "I got to tie up your tootsies, too, lady?" He waggled the knife slowly. "Hog tie you?" He stood over her, grinning wide.

Howls suddenly pulsed from Sarah's throat as she shook her head, the only part left free of bungee wrap.

Hillary held her feet still. Got to keep them free. "Mel! She wants to give you her side. Can't you see?"

He cocked his chin and looked over at Sarah, then back at Hillary. "Nope, she's got nothing more to say. Had her chance. I told her to stand firm, but she caved in to the globals. Forced me to go out alone and slay the giants." He snorted. "Nothing I want to hear anymore."

Hillary's heart hammered. "Why wrap her so tight?"

He stared at Sarah. "Tight? Let me show you tight." He walked over and released the top hook of the bungee, unwrapped it a couple of wraps and stretched it out long into the basement air. Sarah breathed in, raising her chest, but on her exhale, the butcher wrapped the quarter-inch elastic cord around her torso even tighter. Where there had been four wraps from hips up to shoulders, there were now five. He turned back to Hillary.

"Can't you tell what I'm doing? Our Sarah would know if she'd paid the kind of attention we needed to save Stoney's."

"What do you mean?" Hillary asked.

He poured more brandy into the glass. "Let's not waste it this time. It's precious. Made by my father. Tree's right out back in our yard." He held the glass in the palm of his hand and swirled the liquid around, staring into it. "He liked to serve it at sixty-five degrees, for best aroma and flavor, but I think it's colder than that down here now." He swallowed it all himself. "No one 'preciates what I had to do to get the message going. No one."

Neither Sarah nor Hillary made a sound. Rain hammered against the high basement windows.

"You have no clue, do you?" he said.

Hillary shook her head.

"In the 40s and 50s, after the war, Delta farm widows were too squeamish to kill their own birds." He poured himself more brandy.

"Father made up a portable slaughter pack, got to bleed them or you'll ruin the meat. She should have known that much." He glared at Sarah, then stood and rewrapped her. Six wraps this time. Tears rolled down the widow's cheeks.

"But with people—" he leered into Sarah's face "—we don't care about the meat, do we, my pretty? I ever tell you, you look like Mother sometimes? Smell like her, too." He rested his head on her shoulder.

While he was absorbed in tormenting Sarah, Hillary tapped her foot around under her chair and felt the closed umbrella. With the toe of her right shoe, she slid the sword-like umbrella forward toward the back of her left heel, trying to get it wedged between her feet.

Mel rambled as if on stage, performing. "I had to leave a neat display with that damn Brookfield and John, too, so the shoppers wouldn't be put off by a bloody mess. So they'd feel inclined toward what I'm trying to show them. I was always good at PR for Stoney's." He lurched over to shelves stacked with canned fruit in glass jars and pulled out a huge one from the back. "Ever meet Brookfield face to face? The big-time manager?" Strutting around the damp basement, he thrust the wide-mouth gallon jar toward Sarah first and then Hillary. The grayish head—a length of masking tape curling at the edges still in place over his mouth—jiggled in the clear liquid. Two pale blue eyes stared blind out into the basement.

"Say 'Howdy,' ladies." He laughed like a maniac. "He can't greet you back, sorry about that." He shook the jar so the head bobbled. "Nor see you either, although left him with his eyes wide open. At last."

Hillary squeezed her eyes shut and clenched her teeth to keep from screaming. There was no one to hear, anyway. She didn't want to chance sending him over the top.

He set the big jar back on the shelf and pulled out a smaller quart size jar that held a heart the size of his fist. "Here's your sweetheart, Sarah, remember him?"

Sarah squealed from deep in her throat.

"Yes, your partner in crime." He roared with a mad laugh. "You two cowards!"

Sarah's head slumped forward in a faint. Hillary's stomach heaved. She bit her tongue until she could taste blood, forcing herself not to throw up.

The butcher put the Mason jar with the heart back onto the shelf and shoved it toward the back. "They're neighbors, now, those two." He gave the jars a half dozen gentle pats, fondling the smooth glass. "Yup, helping me out but not enough yet. The public's got to notice the killing going on over at the monster store, got to stop feeding those greedy bastards."

Faint whines drifted from Sarah, whose head still drooped onto her chest.

"I never wanted it to come this far." He approached Sarah, bent over and nuzzled his cheek against hers. "I begged you and John not to give up on my meat counter, but you turned around and gave up the whole store. Thought you'd be safe in the arms of the giants."

Breathing heavily, he picked a slim boning knife off his workbench and whirled back and forth, dancing over to press it to the front of Sarah's shoulder, between the second and third bungee wraps, where her arm touched her breast.

"Did you ever look close at their chickens? Those PriceCuts birds you sold us out for? See how the bone splinters cling to the flesh? That's what happens when you cut frozen meat with a band saw. Ragged all around." He leered at her. "The cuts I'll give you'll be a reminder of the polished job you get from a true craftsman. A reminder to others later on."

Umbrella at the ready, Hillary began deliberately coughing. "I could use more brandy, Mel. I'm soaked."

He wheeled around. "You aren't even supposed to be here, you rotten reporter." He stood with his knife raised, looking like a demented Statue of Liberty in the dim basement light.

"Mel, stop demonizing PriceCuts. Take responsibility. You could start over, you and Sarah. Open a small market, maybe east, up in the Sierras where developers haven't thought to mess around yet."

"It's too late. Too late for me and too late for us all." He raised the knife high like a torch. "It's not just PriceCuts. The other bigs are coming here, taking over our little town and the valley with it. Here's to—"

"Mel, let's drink to the way it was. Bring me some brandy. It was the best I've ever tasted." Hillary clenched the umbrella between her feet, frantic that Sarah would suffocate unless unwrapped soon. Hillary'd gathered her courage and felt she could battle him now. And win, too.

His face relaxed. She had him off guard now. He put down the knife and poured more brandy into his glass.

"How about giving her some, too, Mel, for old times' sake?" Hillary nodded toward Sarah, whose eyes widened. She keened a high muted note through the terrycloth stuffed into her mouth.

Mel set his glass on the workbench, got out two empty glasses, and sloshed brandy into them. Rain howled outside and flashes of lightening flickered strobe-like along the walls of the basement. The green flyers were growing dark with moisture from ground water seeping into the concrete basement.

"Here's to the good old days." He approached the wall of flyers and studied it, then pulled one off, waving it like a flag. "The way it was when ordinary people mattered, when global corporations hadn't started cutting prices to chop our lives into pieces." He returned to Sarah and unlatched her top bungee hook. "For a last toast, the way we did that day we signed our first contract in the back room. The day you drew up your flyers. Greenbacks, you called them, Sarah, when you were young and spunky. Clever to make them the color of Monopoly money. Now look at them, all mildewed and forgotten. Monopolies are small change compared to the globals."

He rubbed the pale green paper over Sarah's cheeks as if powdering them, then reached his fingers in to slide the terrycloth gag down onto her chest. He unwound the bungee several wraps and freed her arms, bound so tight with her palms pressed against her chest like chicken wings, she didn't move them even when free of the wraps. "Remember how my parents warned us? Greenbacks. Green. Greed. Get it?" His words slipped out fast, like coins pouring out of a bag.

Sarah's chest heaved, gasping for air.

"Take it," ordered Mel, picking up a glass and thrusting it toward her hands. She wiggled her fingers slightly and whimpered without reaching for the brandy.

"I'm ready. Give her a minute. Bring some to me first, please." Hillary positioned the umbrella in a pincer vice between her feet, waiting for him to come into striking range.

Shakespeare's father was a butcher and the young William exercised his father's trade, "but when he killed a Calf he would do it in a high style, and make a speech."
—*John Aubrey: Brief Lives*

FORTY-NINE

Maniacal Speech

HILLARY COULD BARELY MAKE OUT the words as Sarah began humming and muttering. "Rub dub dub, men in tub, who you think—"

"You have no right," Mel shouted. He froze to the spot as she kept going.

"Butcher, baker..." Sarah whispered. "Mama, kid, smiles . . ."

He didn't so much as blink.

"She 'shamed." Her voice sounded so faint Hillary wasn't certain what she was saying. Hillary worked at the nylon cords binding her hands, grateful he'd left her feet untied.

"Proud, proud, proud," he roared back. "I'm doing this to honor what she believed. She's helpless now, out there in the cemetery by Father. You've got it all wrong."

"Proud back then," she breathed.

Hillary was astonished to see him release the glass he'd held up for Sarah, allowing it to crash to the concrete floor and shatter into wet shards. He staggered over near the workbench and collapsed onto the futon, his head curled toward his knees, arms folded across his chest, hands hugging himself.

"Rub dub dub, men in tub," Sarah chanted, her voice growing stronger as he lay in a fetal position, inert.

He moaned and twisted on the futon, each sound from her sparking a howl out of him.

"Who you think . . . they are?" It was a miracle she had any breath left.

"You know who they are, damn you," he screamed as he sprang up. Hillary prayed he wouldn't go berserk and kill Sarah before she could put her plan into action. He fumbled around among his knives on the workbench, picking up one after another and flinging each so it landed point down, stuck in the soft wood surface. "My father, your John, and me. Who cared about candlestick makers? The butcher was the best of them all. Made us feel satisfied, she did. No woman could match Mother and what she did for a man."

Sarah switched songs, dropping a single word at a time into the damp basement air. "You. Are. My. Sun. Shine. My. Only. Sun."

He lurched over to the light switch and snapped it off, standing in the dark, breathing hard. Hillary blinked, trying to focus by the slim threads of moonlight from the high windows. *Holy Mary. How can I aim in the dark?*

Abandoning words, Sarah hummed one slow note at a time in what remained of her voice.

He snapped the light back on, walked over to the cabinet, uncorked another bottle, and tipped it to his lips, letting it flow freely, brandy sloshing out the sides of his mouth, glaring at Sarah. "No shunshine for Mother now, underground in that wooden box right next to Father. I'm not going to sell this land no matter how much they offer. 'Velopers have to kill me to get it. Souls to the devil, greedy guts. And yours, too." He waved his bottle in Sarah's direction like a salute. "I know you thought to sell and move away to be with your kids. Chicken!"

"Mel," Hillary screamed. "Where's my brandy?"

His breathing sounded like Darth Vader's. He glared at his long-time neighbor who kept up faint melodies as he took another few sloppy swallows from his bottle. Hillary felt a surge of hope mixed with fear as the brandy seemed to be taking effect— he was getting drunk. Weak. He ranted on. "Sarah, you're worsh than John. Selling out now he's gone. Let 'velopers put up ticky-tacky. Our street's turning into a graveyard now—dead to make way for green, green growth. Only greenbacks matter to the greedy honchos. Got yours, won't get mine."

Sarah's eyes were shut but faint notes of "Rub-a-dub-dub" began piping from her throat.

"Mel," Hillary screamed, "It's not her fault! There's still time to save it all!" Hillary worked at the nylon cords binding her wrists, fingering the silky fibers, twisting against their knots.

He pulled a slim knife from the workbench surface and started rubbing it in small circles on a whetstone set onto the old wood surface, staring at Hillary with narrowed eyes. "Past's down the drain, Mom-and-Pops, and you don't care, do you, writer lady? Only make up stories." He shook his head and pursed his lips into a tight O, then turned to Sarah.

"Here come new houses, topper to killing our living. You too. You didn't fight them. John was Pop, you were Mom—let us down."

Sarah gazed at him from under drooping eyelids. "She wouldn't approve, Mel. She was your doting mama, but you didn't know her like I did," she said, her voice so hoarse it was hardly understandable. Hillary didn't know where she got her spunk. "She didn't care about the shop, Mel, not even about your dad, only about you, her darling boy, the one who survived."

"You're lying. The shop was the world to her, him too. A mercy Father was hit by a Mack truck in the fog, years before a hint of PriceCuts. Ha! KillCuts, name of their game." He stood clenching the knife for a few seconds then let it fall to the rough wood surface as he turned to face the back yard. "I never found a woman like her." Swaying, he hugged his arms around himself and moaned from deep in his throat. "Looked, but none good enough."

"Mel, your mother wanted you to grow up as a living savior, not a killer." Sarah's voice rang strong and clear.

"Savior?"

"She wanted you to marry and birth butchers as saviors."

"What you talking?"

"Her whole family, butchered by the Nazis, right in front of her toddler eyes. Her way to keep from being slaughtered was to link herself with men who could cut anything and everything except her—underneath it all she was terrified and would be if she were here now, beside you. Didn't you think she went overboard in her cheerleading for you and your father? It was women she felt safe with, women like me."

Silence filled the cold room, the downpour outside slowing to steady drips that slid down the tin rain gutters to splat against concrete pads near the house.

Melvin grabbed his knife and moved over to Sarah, the steely knife tip glinting as he poked it against her throat. "She was safe with me." He scowled. "But, you're not."

FIFTY

A Thrust

HILLARY'S EFFORTS to free herself from the ropes caused scrabbling sounds as the nylon cords slipped to the floor. Mel rushed over, straddling her chair to grab the ropes fallen to the ground. She clamped her feet around the orange umbrella, aimed it upward, and thrust hard, huffing out a powerful "kee-yah!"

The umbrella rammed home, stabbing him in the testicles with its chrome tip. With a howl, he crumpled to the concrete. "You bitch," he gasped, his legs in a fetal position, hands cupping his groin.

Hillary knew she had to work fast. In a flash, she jumped up to release Sarah's bungee cords, and clenching the springy elastics, wheeled back toward Melvin, bungee hooks flailing the air. Hillary wrapped the cord around his ankles, still pressed together in agony over the insult to his manhood. She stretched the bungee up and around his neck, wrapping it twice, nearly strangling him in the process. Then she fastened the hook over itself at the back of his neck.

"How's that for hog tied, mister? And with your own bungees!" She ran to Sarah, who had crumpled toward the floor.

At that moment, Roger and Matt broke open the back door into the basement. Matt had his pepper spray out and aimed at Mel, who was writhing against the restraints of the bungee and the lingering effect of Hillary's assault with the orange umbrella.

Sirens wailed, marking the arrival of Ed, Walt, and deputies, who came in through the back door, surrounded the mad butcher and handcuffed him. Huffing and puffing, Ed and Walt lifted him off the ground and taking one arm each, escorted him kicking and moaning out the back basement door.

Paramedics ran in and assessed Sarah, placed her on a stretcher and gave her oxygen before taking her out. Hillary staggered to the workbench and collapsed on Melvin's futon.

FIFTY-ONE

Thanksgiving

MORNING SUNLIGHT spilled though bare branches in the Morada forest and cast spiky shadows on Hillary's cottage walls. When she'd checked her Powerbook for email, one message stood out as if written in neon—the Subject line: "Hillary a Hero????" It was from Charles. Finally.

News stories on Melvin Hermann had carried Roger's byline, and set out Hillary's daring rescue of Sarah. Hillary detested being the subject of the news instead of reporting it. From the email subject line, it looked like it was her frantic race to get Sarah out of danger that had provoked Charles into action and not any of the earlier stories she had written. *Holy Mary, help me now.* Then she noticed the name in the cc: line. It was the head of the Clearwater College English Department chair.

She could not open herself to this today. Could not. Would not. She shut down the Powerbook.

She was determined to get on with throwing what she had called an "early bird" Thanksgiving feast, grateful to have Melvin behind bars and Sarah still alive. Ed had come midmorning to help with the meal. Hillary wondered how it made him feel that he had arrived after she had already incapacitated Melvin. And even after Roger and Matt showed up. She sensed it was too touchy a subject for her to bring up at this stage of their relationship. Ed seemed content today, puttering around the kitchen, as shadows slid down the wall toward noontime.

Hillary answered the knock at the door to welcome Roger, who'd picked up Sarah, only a few days out of the hospital. "Come on in! And relax— no flesh to carve today—I've got a tofu turkey in the oven, a "Tofurky."

Sarah moved stiffly toward the bright kitchen and opened the oven door just a crack, checking out the shape of the ersatz bird in the hot interior. "That water he left on running over my chicken, you know, honey?" She nodded at Hillary. "It ran for hours—my water bill was sky high! I'm not complaining though," she smiled, "but I'm ready to give up meat for good." She hobbled over to sit by the fireplace. "Can't get warm enough anymore."

Roger served her a cup of hot Cider Jack and added another log to the fire.

In the kitchen, Ed inhaled deeply, over the simmering pot of potato soup Hillary'd made that morning. "My Irish ancestors lived on spuds. You can give it a stir," she told him, smiling.

He poked around in her pottery jug of wooden kitchen tools and picked out a spoon carved into a twisted design.

"That's a Welsh Love Spoon." She glanced at him. "I got it on a trip to the UK after college, Eddie."

"Speaking of Welsh and names," he said, "my given name's actually Odgar, Welsh for the Old English Edgar. It means 'wealthy spear' of all crazy things." He laughed and plunged the spoon into the potato soup.

She began peeling more potatoes, their skins falling helter-skelter onto a torn-open brown bag from Morada Market. "We need them for the mashed, too." She felt safe and happy with Eddie around but not sure where they were headed. *What do I want? Warmth to fill the gaps left by Daddy's death? Information about my long-missing mother? Forgiveness for using others' words?* No one out here had discovered her shameful secret, but now she had to figure out how to deal with Charles.

One thing she knew for sure was that the passion driving Melvin's crimes had reached her. It was wrong to kill people to drive home his message. But she got it. And she was going to weave the validity of his rage, if not his murders, into the first-person story she was working on now, an exclusive for *The Acorn.*

When they were seated at the table, Eddie offered a brief thanks for bringing them all safely to this late autumn day. He added his gratitude for Hillary's potato soup, winking at her from his place at the head of the table. Her heart melted at his allusion to the story from his childhood.

She scooped up a ladleful of creamy soup and held it high. "In honor of our survival, no knives carving meat are allowed at this table—today, we are a house of spoons and forks. Amen," she shouted, satisfied to be alive and all in one piece, with these good friends in Northern California's Central Valley. Tomorrow would be another day.

THE END

ACKNOWLEDGMENTS

In exploring the dark side of human nature—to balance my goodie two-shoes upbringing—I'm grateful for the inspiration of Donna Tartt, Jeff Lindsey, Thomas Harris, and Dean Koontz. For the seed idea of *House of Cuts*, I am indebted to the *Los Angeles Times* owners and minions for their series of Golden Handshakes in the 1990s, which revealed the deadly impact of big business on the little people.

Hugs and high fives to my readers and cheerleaders over the years it's taken to bring *House of Cuts* to publication: Jacki and Jan, Julie and Karen, Toni and Lucy, Tori and Sylvia, and my buddies KT and NS. Writing groups and conferences have been vital as well, including Sisters in Crime and the Gold Rush Writers Conference. Some of my best writing students have been great supporters, too, such as Carl M. I am grateful for positive feedback early in the book's process from C. Michael Curtis—fiction editor at *Atlantic Monthly*—at one of Zoe Keithley's terrific workshops.

ABOUT THE AUTHOR

A native of California, June Gillam focuses on issues that bridge the light and the darkness of this journey we call life. Her poems have been published in regional outlets, with her first poetry collection, *So Sweet Against Your Teeth*, now in print. After she realized many of her poems wanted to be stories, she began writing short fiction and is published in venues such as *Metal Scratches* and *America's Intercultural Magazine*. Now she's working on a series of novels featuring Hillary Broome, a redheaded reporter in her mid-thirties who writes for a Central California paper and serves as the journalism advisor at a local community college. Visit the author at her website:
www.junegillam.com.

WHAT'S NEXT

In the Hillary Broome Series

HOUSE OF DADS opens in December of 2005 during the peak of the housing construction boom, when Hillary's cousin Theodore Broome, heir to the most powerful real estate development corporation in California, collapses and dies at an Irish wake, drawing Hillary into a network of jealousy, greed, and secrets that could topple financial empires and wipe out family corporations.

In the midst of deciding whether or not to marry detective Ed Kiffin, Hillary must find out if cousin Teddy's death was an accident or fratricide—the outcome of passive-aggressive sibling rivalry—aimed from his twin sister Violet, who is willing to kill her own mother to protect her newfound power in Broome Construction Corporation, control of which passed to her at Teddy's death. Buffeted by uncovering shocking family secrets, Hillary must stop Violet from committing matricide that could spill over and put Hillary's life in danger, as well.